EMBER RUSSELL

Soulless

Creemore Series Book One

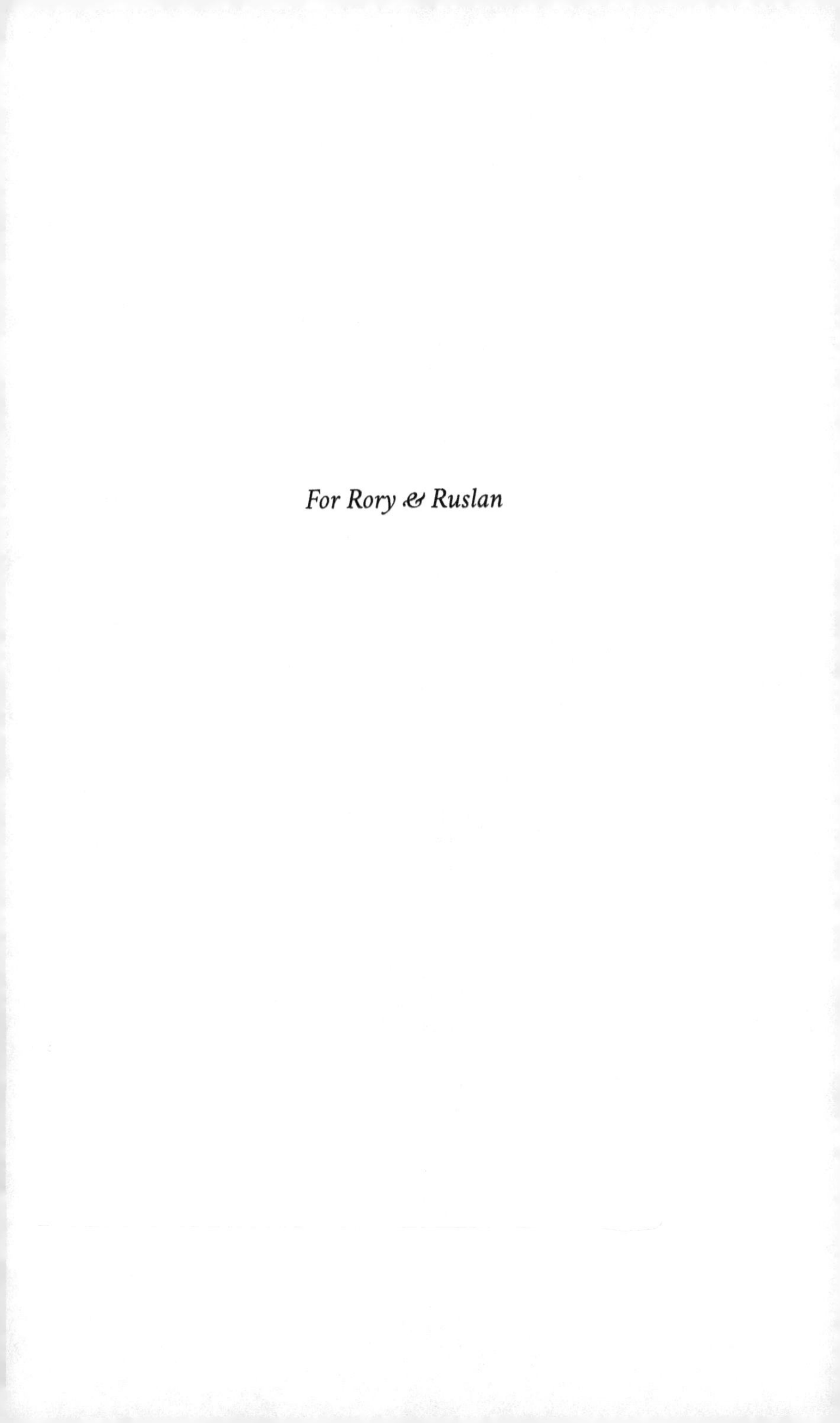

For Rory & Ruslan

Contents

Chapter 1

The echoing sounds of distant gunfire and screaming faded from my sleep-addled mind. I opened my tired eyes to see new water stains on the ceiling, mocking me. The recent rainstorms must have been too much for the roof, again. In the low morning light of my bedroom, I closed my eyes again and calculated the repair cost.

Yep, that was going to cost a lot of money. Money I did not have.

"All right, Kit, let's do this," I moaned, turning to my furry bed companion. "Time for coffee," I said as I heaved myself up off the old brass bed. Like much of the furniture in the dilapidated house, the bed was old and falling apart. On better days, I would call it charming; today in the small drafty hours of the morning, I would call it uncomfortable and cold. It was spring, but winter was clinging on, unwilling to let go.

Kit eyed me through half-closed eyes before huffing and burying herself further into her makeshift nest of blankets. You'd think, as a young two-tailed fox shifter, she would be energetic and ready to go—but not Kit; she was notoriously slow to get up in the morning. I patted what I could see of her tiny orange head. For someone the size of a shoebox, she still took up well over half the bed.

Ignoring Kit and her much better idea of going back to sleep, I reached for an oversized flannel shirt and sweatpants to ward off the damp chill. I headed down the hall toward the ancient kitchen, sparing a glance at myself in the hallway mirror. My long auburn hair looked like a hurricane had swept through it in the night. The green paint on my pale, freckled face was probably the surest sign a shower was in order this morning. I looked like a renovation Barbie that had been microwaved on high. I chuckled to myself at the thought—I didn't even own a microwave.

The smell of coffee brewing led me to the kitchen. The previous month I had splurged on a fancy coffee machine, which turned itself on in the morning, an extravagant expense I did not regret. I flicked on the lights, briefly admiring my work before grabbing a mug. The kitchen was mostly renovated with dark sage-green paint, white cabinets, and new stainless-steel appliances. A dark wood butcher-block island and wooden stools took up most of the large space. This room had taken the last month to come together; it was finally looking like a functional kitchen again.

After a rather abrupt end to my career in the armed forces, this house had been an impulse purchase. Both Kit and I needed somewhere to land quickly and lick our wounds in peace. I had bought it sight-unseen through a local broker and on the recommendation of a friend who lived nearby. We had arrived in Creemore with the dirt of the Middle East still in our hair.

Gazing over the fields behind the house as the sun rose, it was hard not to be glad I'd bought the time and money-sucking beast. After leaving the military three years before, I had poured all my savings into restoring the old house on the hill, to turn it into a short-term boarding house. I wasn't having much success with the boarding element of my plan, having only one renter currently, but the renovations were going well. I looked at the positives, not my dwindling bank balance.

Located just outside of Creemore, we were sandwiched between Collingwood, with its sweeping mountains prime for skiing in the winter, and the beaches of Lake Huron. Strangely, it was also one of the few places where magic users of various types outnumbered humans. The exact reason for this unique phenomenon had never been satisfactorily explained to me. With all the varied people moving through the village, you'd think it would be an easy sell, but with the house only half-done, it seemed to put people off. I was rushing to get everything up to snuff before running out of money in a few months. Even if we had to give up the house next season, I didn't think we would leave the strange little village. For the most part, humans and magic users lived well enough together. Still, as a hedge witch and veteran, who was carrying around a traumatized fox shifter, it would be hard to fit in anywhere. Creemore, with all its eccentricities, suited us. I told people we had come there for Kit, to help her heal, but I think we'd both found some peace there.

The coffee maker sputtered as the last drop of the black elixir of happiness into the pot. Grabbing my chipped mug, I poured myself a cup of coffee, black – because why dilute the caffeine? Searching around for my coat, I navigated the paint cans and drop cloths to the front porch. Slipping on my jacket, I kicked open the sticky front door. Spring had warmed the ground, and it was just starting to thaw the last of the snow from the winter. The birds were chirping; today was going to be a good day. I was going to tile the floor, install the pendant lights… the smell of rotting meat derailed my optimistic to-do list.

Looking toward the front of the yard, where my nose already told me something was amiss, was a colossal head impaled on a stick and mounted in the middle of the front yard.

"Well, shit," I said to myself. Today would not be the day I finished the kitchen tiles.

Chapter 2

I heard the door creak softly behind me. "Morning, Abby," I said without taking my eyes off the decapitated head that was surely going to ruin my day, perhaps even my week. While I was no stranger to violence, I was not okay with having any sort of anything impaled on my front lawn like a grim Halloween decoration.

Abby was my one and only boarder; she arrived mysteriously a week after us and had been here ever since. A tall, willowy woman, she could have been anywhere between eighteen and eighty. Her timeless face was pale, with wide grey eyes and light blue hair. Even in yellow bunny pyjamas, she carried herself with regal grace. She had told me when she arrived that her appearance resulted from a glamour charm, her true form being something that not even the quirky village of Creemore would appreciate. She avoided all talk of her past but was an unapologetic gossip, regaling me with stories of the occupants of our small village. I was glad of her presence. She wielded a paintbrush like a woman possessed, and with her biting humour and quick wit, she was always good company. Over the past few years, I had counted her as one of my closest friends; we both respected each other's desire to leave the past in the past and forge new lives here.

Her soft voice came from beside me. "Hmmm."

I turned to her. "That's all you've got? Head on a pole, and I get an unconcerned 'Hmmm?'"

I shot her a look full of tired exasperation as I collapsed down into one of the worn wicker chairs that adorned the wide front porch. Taking a large gulp of my coffee, already planning the second one I was going to need now. Decapitated Head on a Stick was not the lawn ornament I had in mind for the front yard. I was a more Ironic-looking Lawn Gnome Placed in Inappropriate Poses sort of person.

Abby wandered over to the offending cranium, picking up a stick along the gravel pathway. Holding up the branch, she took a tentative poke at the head. A bog fly took off, affronted by the interruption from its meal.

"Well, it's dead," she said, poking it once more for good measure. "Yes, certainly very dead." Turning, Abby headed back up the gravel path to take a seat on the wooden front steps. "I think it's small for a demon head, though. It is rather disappointing."

"You and I have very different opinions about what constitutes a disappointment. Finding the box of cookies empty is disappointing. Demon head on a pole, regardless of size, not so much." I sat up in my chair. "Wait, are you sure it's a demon head?" I said, my brain finally catching up with her words.

Demons will turn to ash and return to whichever hell they came from within an hour or two of being killed, depending on how powerful they were. A severed head should have been long gone by now. By the smell, I would guess that the head had been removed from its owner quite some time ago. I slouched back down in my chair, relaxing somewhat; a demon was much easier to deal with. Rather than facing a nefarious murder mystery, I was merely looking at an inconvenient demon head on my lawn. Killing demons was perfectly legal here and unofficially encouraged by the Magic Council. While it didn't solve the mystery of how it got here or who had brought us such an unwelcome gift, it simplified things slightly.

Abby paused, as if considering my question, looking back toward our new lawn ornament. "Yes, quite sure. The demon tattoo on the forehead is quite clear—from one of the lower hells if I'm not mistaken." She turned to me, looking contemplative. "What will you do with it?"

"Finish my coffee, then probably call Alrick, I guess," I said, shrugging. "This isn't really my jurisdiction." While it wasn't technically illegal, it would interest Alrick.

Alrick was the Magic Council's local representative for our area, based in Toronto. He was an overly serious man who made a point to memorize the council's procedural happenings like a fanatic. He had approached me last year about being the county representative for the township. The Clearview Township Magic Council Deputized Local Representative is a long title with very few responsibilities and an even smaller salary. However, I was in no position to decline; the house required a steady income stream to keep the renovations on track. In the year since I had taken over the job, there hadn't been a lot for me to do. The only "enforcement" I'd had to do was a stern telling-off of a bunch of creative teens. They had enchanted a tractor, taking it for a joyride all over the village before parking it on the roof of the church. Alrick would know what the procedure was for abandoned demon heads that were stubbornly persistent at existing. My official procedure book was propping open the basement steps at that moment and thus indisposed; besides, this was way above my pay grade.

Abby turned to ponder the head once more. "Interesting." She mused, rising from the steps with the grace of a ballerina and silently disappeared into the house. I shook my head at her comment - that woman was a strange one, 'interesting', was not the first word to come to my mind.

Taking the last sip of my now cold coffee, I pulled out my cellphone and texted Alrick the details and a quick photo of my new lawn ornament. The responsibility now transferred. I contemplated my empty mug and the possibility of breakfast. Before I could summon the motivation to propel myself up out of the chair, the front door opened to reveal a sleepy-looking Kit. Abby followed behind, carrying scones and steaming mugs of coffee on a makeshift platter of leftover plywood. Did I mention how much I loved Abby? Kit padded her way out to her favourite spot on the front porch, part laundry basket, part dog bed. Before she could get comfortable, she hesitated, sniffing the air. She looked around furiously before having a sneezing attack that landed her on her rump, looking rather undignified. Locating the offensive smell's source, she shot me an annoyed look, as if I had somehow deliberately put the head on the lawn to insult her delicate sensibilities.

"What? I didn't put it there," I replied to her unspoken outrage.

With a disgruntled huff, Kit snatched a scone off the clearly amused Abby's makeshift tray. With tail and nose in the air, she scuttled quickly into the house without further comment.

Abby handed me a mug of coffee and a scone, having the decency to at least try to hide her amused grin. Kit was a diva, and Abby was often a bystander of our strange dynamic. I imagined it must be pretty entertaining for her to watch. We sat in companionable silence while I mentally prepared myself for removing Mr Head from his perch on the pole. I hoped that referring to it as Mr Head would make this a marginally less grotesque task. A loud pop suddenly interrupted my mental preparations, followed by a crash and angry grunting.

Abby jumped up, startled, and pulled a dagger from her pyjama pocket, brandishing it like a warrior ready for battle. My boarder carrying a blade carrying a blade, a rather sharp looking one, was something to note. I would definitely follow up on that later. What kind of trouble was she expecting to face in her adorable yellow bunny pyjamas?

Looking at her panicked face, this was probably not the time for bunny jokes. "It's okay, Abby, it's Alrick," I said in what I hoped was a calm voice. "He's a teleport mage—just not a very good one. Terrible aim… it sounds like he's landed in the rose bushes." I smiled at my friend. "Let's put the dagger down and go save him from the roses."

Abby relaxed somewhat and tucked the dagger away swiftly, nodding her assent.

"I think we should probably talk about why you need to have a dagger in your cute bunny pyjamas."

She frowned, looking confused. "These are cute? I thought they were a food theme, like your pizza pyjamas. Do you not eat rabbits?" She looked down at her outfit. "I don't think I want 'cute' clothing if it means I can't carry a blade."

I snorted, not even sure where to begin with that conversation. Untangling Abby's logic could wait until later. First, I needed to rescue Alrick.

We followed the unintelligible cursing sounds to find a small balding man in a brown suit losing an argument with the roses. Abby grabbed him by the collar, hoisting him out of the offending bush, and unceremoniously dumped him on the grass. Turning to me, she said, "If you'll excuse me, I need to go change now," and moved swiftly back to the front of the house.

Assessing the heap of brown suit and comb-over on the grass, I took pity on the man and helped him to his feet.

Once upright, he looked up at me with a furious expression. "Alena Maisie MacKenzie! What is the meaning of this! A demon head! On a pole!" Without pausing for breath, Alrick carried on, reaching a new pitch of hysterics. "What have you done to stir up trouble? My county has a perfect record! You've ruined it! Who texts at seven in the morning?! This is not the correct procedure! Don't you know how to use a phone like a civilized person?!" Panting, he bent over, putting his hand on his knees.

I regarded Alrick while he gathered his composure. He was a man of many words, usually colourful and loudly expressed. His appearance did not match the man's ability to reprimand even the most experienced council members. Every part of him was a shade of brown: brown leathery skin, large brown eyes, a brown tie with an ill-fitting suit that looked like something stolen out of a 1970s car salesperson's wardrobe. Suppressing a cringe at hearing my full name shouted at a volume customarily reserved for yodelling, I waited for him to finish his tirade.

Taking a deep breath, Alrick stood up to his full height and pulled his shoulders back. "Well then, let's see this so-claimed head on a pole that you so rudely awoke me for."

He started down the grass lawn toward the front fence. I hurried after him like a chastened child, hoping this would not take the rest of the day; I had tiles to lay.

"It's a demon head," Alrick stated matter-of-factly while

poking it with a pen.

"Yes," I said.

"It smells quite old; someone must have brought it here from elsewhere." He nodded to himself. "But why would they do that? Yes, yes, very interesting."

"Yes…" I nodded.

"Should be ash by now—very unusual indeed."

"Yes," I repeated, feeling like I wasn't really required to participate in this conversation.

"Can I take some of it back with me?" he asked, turning to me. "This is a serious business, Miss MacKenzie. I expect you to be more professional! You are the Clearview Township Magic Council Deputized Local Representative—appearances must be maintained!" He waved his pen in my face. "I will expect a full report on my desk within the customary three days, as well as all the required paperwork." He listed off the forms I would need.

My attention drifted away. Of course—paperwork. There was always paperwork, I thought, groaning inwardly.

"I'll get back to you if I need anything else, but I suggest you hold on to the specimen in case it's required for further investigation. Though I would say remove it from its current location—the aesthetic is off-putting," he said, giving the head a long look. "Good day, Miss MacKenzie." And with a loud pop, he was gone.

Somewhat bewildered, I strode off toward the shed to find a bucket to house my guest, Mr Head. This was, after all, a boarding house, though I felt like he would bring me more trouble than rent.

Chapter 3

Splattered in paint and plaster, I finally plopped down at the newly restored kitchen counter. After all the excitement that morning, I had still managed to finish the tiles and the final paint touch up. Glancing around, I was pleased with the progress the old house was making. Kit nudged my leg gently. Pulling her up from the floor, I asked, "What do you think, Kit?" She nodded once, which I took for approval. "Time for a beer, I think." Setting Kit down, I headed for the shower to get cleaned up before heading out in search of food and drink.

Kit started hissing behind me in the front hall.

"Kit? What's wrong?" I asked, seeing her hackles raised. She looked at me once before skittering away up the stairs. Before I had a chance to follow, I heard the sounds of a car coming up the drive. Peering out the window, I saw a black SUV speeding up the long driveway and coming to an abrupt halt in a shower of gravel and dust.

Oh, please be a potential boarder, I thought as I headed outside to the porch and put on my best "this is a happy, amazing home, please give me money" face. Stepping out into the late afternoon sun, I shielded my eyes, trying to get a better glimpse at our prospective new lodger.

The man who climbed out of the SUV took my breath away. He stalked across the lawn toward me like a conqueror who would be more at home defending Wakanda than the backwoods of Canada. He was tall and lean, his ebony skin smooth and enticing. His crisp black suit clung to his broad shoulders, promising that what lay beneath would be solid and powerful.

"Are you Alena Maisie MacKenzie?" His voice was rich and smooth, with just a hint of a London accent. It was the second time that day I'd heard my full name, but this time it gave me shivers. My repressed and neglected sex drive sat up and took notice of the man in front of me. I probably needed to get out more. I mentally shook myself. I was acting like a teenager in front of a stranger.

"Ummm… yep, yep, that's me." I beamed back at him. Smooth Alena, so smooth. Not awkward at all.

He looked me over in all my paint and plaster glory. With my long hair, pert nose, and eyes the colour of a stormy sea, I was far from ugly. Something like surprise flashed across his expression before being quickly smothered, and he went back to regarding me impassively.

"Show me the head," he demanded.

"Excuse me?" My mind had drifted into several scenarios, none of which involved decapitated heads. I had lost track of the conversation briefly.

He reached up to remove his sunglasses and held out his hand in greeting. "Marcus Friedrich, MCIB. The council sent me to investigate the demon head."

Snapping back to the conversation at hand, I looked up at him, finally noticing what I had missed. My breath caught in my chest, but this time it was a very different sort of feeling. He wore binding tattoos. The three black tattooed rings around his wrist had the effect of a bucket of ice water being dropped on my head, freezing my internal teenager solid. He was a bound soulless.

Not much was known about the soulless. A Soulless was the product of a joining of angel and vampire. They were part of vampire society, and the ones that were not mercenaries were the unofficial army of the vampires. The Soulless were bound at birth with magic tattoos to control the warring nature of being both light and dark magic, and the only way they could break the bindings and become whole was to find the other half of their soul in another soulless. The legends had always sounded like overly romantic nonsense to me. Still, I knew for sure that they were clinically logical, ruthless, powerful, and, when called for, brutally and efficiently violent. This man was very, very dangerous. I'd never come across one before, but they had briefed us on them as part of our basic training. I knew enough to be very wary of the man standing before me.

Tentatively, I reached out to shake his hand. "Yes, of course, follow me." His skin felt warm and his grip was firm. The attraction I felt earlier returned briefly before I pushed it aside, reminding myself that while he might have looked like a man, he was a predator. I led him around to the back of the house, where I had unceremoniously dumped Mr Head in a discarded paint bucket.

"Here we are," I said, as I pried the lid off the bucket. The smell had not improved over the course of the day.

Marcus stepped forward, pulling out a charm, which he held over the head of the demon. It spun slowly, a glowing glyph.

"An identification charm?" I asked curiously. Identification charms were typically used for things like metal, spelled items, or potions. I had never seen one used on anything living before, or, I suppose more accurately, anything recently dead.

"Of a sort," Marcus replied without looking up.

Intrigued, I leaned over his shoulder while the glyph continued to glow in the air. With a somewhat anticlimactic puff of smoke, the head turned to ash, leaving a faint glow of blue.

"Does that mean what I think it means?" I asked. All magic had a signature; it was always seen as colours either in the person's energy or when they were using it. When I used my magic to help plants grow or brew potions—which was about the extent of it—they would glow a pale green-brown, a sign of earth magic that designated me as a hedge witch. But blue was human. That demon was no demon, but it was clearly marked as a demon. That made no sense at all; something else was going on.

He grunted noncommittally in response, his long strides propelling him toward the SUV.

"Hey, look, what's going on?" I cried after him, hurrying to catch up.

"Magic Council business. I am not at liberty to discuss with civilians," he replied, opening the door to the SUV. He climbed in. "Are you aware of the location of the office of the local representative for this area? I need to make contact and brief them of the situation." He looked down from his SUV, waiting for my answer.

I pointed up to where I had propped open my bedroom window with the ancient laptop that served as my official Magic Council Local Representative "office". Smiling smugly. "I believe the office is on the second floor, third door on the left." Meeting his glare head-on, I asked. "Care to share with the class now?"

"You? You're on the Magic Council?" He looked sceptical, while taking in my dirty coveralls and paint-splattered face.

"I am." I smiled back at him, pleased that this redundant title might actually, finally, be of some use to me. I wanted to know what was going on.

Marcus shrugged. "All right then, is there somewhere we can discuss the case? Perhaps more appropriate than all this." He waved his hand around the uncut grass and somewhat dilapidated porch I had yet to repair.

"I'm going to overlook you insulting my beloved home for the sake of the case. We can head into town and get something to eat while you brief me." I sighed tiredly, the day catching up with me suddenly and no rest in sight from the sounds of it. "First, however, I need to get cleaned up. I guess you can wait here." I mockingly waved my hand around, mimicking his earlier comment about the yard as I headed into the house.

Stripping off the coveralls, followed closely by my shirt, I wandered into my bedroom in just a bra and underwear. I found Kit lying on the bed watching something on the tablet. I paused. An MCIB agent was out front, and Kit wasn't strictly speaking the most legal thing to have in my home. While technically a shifter, she could not shift. Kit's story was a sad one and the primary reason we had come to Creemore. During my final tour in the Middle East, what was supposed to be a peacekeeping mission had turned out to be anything but. We were bombarded constantly, not only by human artillery, but by magical as well.

I tried not to think too hard about the things I had seen. When we had found Kit, she had been in human form. Just a child, really—only nine or ten. She was the only survivor of a horrific magical attack that had levelled an entire village.

When we finally freed her from the rubble, she had awoken briefly—long enough to see the horror surrounding us. The trauma of it had made her shift to her fox form before falling unconscious again. Our unit medical doctor, another shifter, named Becca, and I cared for her as best we could. It was touch and go for a few weeks. She pulled through in the end but had never shifted back to human form no matter what we tried. Under shifter law, she was to be put down if she could not shift. Something about a human mind trapped in an animal's body made shifters go crazy, and they had a tendency to viciously attack others. Becca suggested that if we wanted Kit to survive and have a chance, she should be relocated somewhere, and quickly. I applied for my voluntary release request the next day, and three years later, here we were. Kit still couldn't shift, but she seemed happier. Some days, like today, she acted more human, watching TV and eating chips. Other days she seemed more fox, leaving dead rabbits in the yard. I called it progress. It was okay with me whatever path Kit chose. Some wounds don't heal, as I well understood.

"Kit," I said tentatively, "there's an MCIB agent out front. I'm going to go to town to get something to eat with him and talk; it's about the head from this morning—that cool with you?"

Kit huffed at me without looking up from her show.

"Kit." I added some warning to my voice. "Don't let him see you, okay?"

She finally looked up at me with a question in her eyes; worry crossed her tiny face before she nodded once in agreement. She picked up the tablet in her little paws and hopped off the bed, dragging a blanket with her. She gave me a small salute and pushed the tablet and blanket under the bed, following it and swiftly disappearing.

"Hey Kit, I won't let anything happen to you, okay?" I spoke softly, but was sure she could hear me under the bed. "Don't eat all the girl guide cookies again while I'm out; that's just not cool." I turned toward the bathroom and chucked off the rest of my clothes; I heard something that sounded suspiciously like Kit snickering from her blanket fort. My hope faded that I would come home to any cookies. Damn, the mint ones were the best, too. But my mind eased somewhat, feeling that Kit would stay safe. I headed for my long-anticipated shower.

Chapter 4

Not bothering to lock the door, I bounded down the porch steps to meet Marcus in the driveway. I felt more energetic after getting cleaned up, putting a spring in my step as I headed to my beat-up pickup truck. It didn't look like much, but I loved it. Its baby-blue paintwork and chrome accents made it look like something out of a 1950s movie. I had bought it off a retired farmer down the road. He said he had no idea where it came from. It had been in a barn for nearly two decades, hidden under a heap of hay behind assorted farm equipment. It had taken me well over a year to get it running properly. When I was driving the back roads, windows open, blasting Shakira, I felt like there was nothing I couldn't do. Some people did yoga. I drove.

I was brought up short by Marcus's massive frame blocking my path. "I'll drive," he declared in a voice that brooked no argument.

I frowned. That wasn't happening. I would not be trapped in a car with this man. I was clearly going to show him how things worked around here. He was about to get a front-row seat to some world-class stubbornness. Smiling sweetly, I looked up at him with big eyes and fluttering eyelashes.

"Really? Thanks so much, you big powerful man. Lead the

way," I said in the most genuine manner I could muster, patting his muscled arm. Marcus eyed me suspiciously before turning to head toward the SUV. Seizing my opportunity, I dashed toward my truck, jumped in, and turned the ignition over. Before he had time to react, I had peeled out of the driveway. Smiling smugly, I rolled down the window and shoved my head out the window. Honking loudly, I shouted at him, "Come on, slowpoke, you can follow me into the village," and took off down the dirt road. Reaching for my jerry-rigged iPod, I scrolled through the songs. Queen, yes, this situation called for some Queen. Grinning, I headed to Creemore.

Just as the sun was setting, I pulled in front of Dragons Meet. The old pub was part brewery, part pub, part coffee house, based on the time of day and the whims of the owner, Brandon. Brandon and I had crossed paths shortly after I'd come to the village. In my quest for beer and a meal that was not out of a box, I was directed to "the Meet". On the main street in what once was the local gas station, the Meet was something out of a hipster's wet dream, with wooden booths, flannel accents, and vinyl records from unknown artists peppering the plain brick walls. Brandon claimed he was merely an ironic hipster, though I'm still unsure what that even means. The food was good, and the beer was better, so I had become a regular almost immediately.

I leaned against the faded gas meters while I waited for Marcus to finish parking, bracing myself for his anger at my earlier antics. As he approached, he looked more bemused than angry. Well, colour me surprised. Where was all that Soulless repressed rage? He lowered his sunglasses and looked at me with those clear blue eyes. "You are very annoying," he said and walked right past me; I watched as the heavy pub door swallowed him.

Well, that was very unexpected. I followed in Marcus's wake, unable to come up with a witty comeback, and pushed open the heavy oak door to the pub. Inhaling the welcoming scents of food and people, I waved at Brandon and headed to one of the more private booths near the back of the building, where Marcus had already taken a seat.

As I took my seat across from Marcus as Brandon saddled up beside the table.

"Alena, such good timing! I have something new for you."

I cringed. "Why must you experiment on me?" While I complained loudly and often about some of the more questionable brews, I enjoyed his enthusiasm for new beers. I may even have been a bit of a beer snob, if there was such a thing.

"I experiment on you because I can," he said, grinning and handing me a pale-looking ale. "I call this one 'You've never heard of it.'" He set the glass in front of me and turned to Marcus. "And who is your scary but handsome friend?" he said, fluttering his lashes at him.

One of Brandon's more endearing qualities was that he was a vivacious flirt. Once, after a few too many beers, he had chatted up a bar stool before deciding its personality was too wooden to be a romantic partner for him. While he flirted with just about anyone and anything, I'd never actually seen him leave with anyone. He never talked about it, but I got the sense he wasn't ever planning to get seriously involved with anyone again. There was a story there, but I never asked him about it. I understood more than most the desire to forget the past and move on.

"This is Marcus from MCIB; he's here for an investigation,"

I said absently, pondering the glass in front of me while some purple smoke puffed on the surface. "I'll try this, but I'd like to remind you what happened last time you 'experimented' on me." Brandon, being a low-level mage, liked to mix magic into some of his creations with some very mixed results.

Brandon looked hurt. "You were only purple for a day; it wasn't that bad. You said yourself it tasted wonderful! The taste is the most important thing—not side effects." He looked over at Marcus. "So you're here about Alena's demon lawn-lollipop?" he asked. Ah, small towns—news always got around fast. It was a comforting universal constant.

I snorted ungracefully. "Lawn-lollipop? Really?" I said, amused despite myself. Marcus looked annoyed.

"Is it common for you to share sensitive council incidents with the public?" he chastised.

I shrugged. "It's a small town. People talk. A lot."

"Oh, she didn't tell me. I saw it on Facebook!" Brandon piped in, as if somehow this was better. I sighed. The village had a Facebook group that was used to track the happenings of the occupants. When we had first come here, it was alarming to me how quickly news travelled and how little privacy there was. Over the years, I had grown immune to the insanity of it all and learned to just roll with it.

Marcus looked horrified at the thought of his investigation being discussed on social media. Realizing he may have misstepped, Brandon changed topics abruptly. "Can I get you something? I have a stout; it's tall, dark, and so smooth," he said, wiggling his eyebrows suggestively. I rolled my eyes at him. Despite himself, I saw Marcus fighting down the corners of his mouth. It was hard not to like Brandon.

"I'd prefer a red ale if you have one—something bold,"

Marcus replied seriously, with only a hint of humour in his eyes.

Brandon blushed right up from his curly red beard to his bald head. "Ay, sir," he said with a mock salute, and quickly marched off to the bar.

I laughed hard and loud; I think it was the first time I had relaxed enough to laugh since this bizarre day had started. While the day was far from over, laughing was wearing away the edges of my worry. "You have a sense of humour!" I laughed again, astonished; Marcus was not what I had expected.

He smiled back at me, some warmth touching his usually serious features. "I feel things." He hesitated for a moment, as if trying to choose his words carefully. "They are just controlled. We are indeed more emotionally undemonstrative than most other races, but that does not mean the emotions are not there. Sadness, fear, humour, anger." He looked up at me, considering. "It's all there. We are just trained to control it from a young age. Unchecked, they will eat away at the binding magic we endure as the bound soulless." He sat back, leaning against the wooden booth.

Well, that was more information than I had expected from him about the soulless. I was going to have to seriously re-evaluate some of my acquired prejudices. Clearly, I was uninformed.

We sat in companionable silence until Brandon reappeared with Marcus's ale and some meat pies. "I'm going to assume you haven't eaten today, Alena," he said with mock scorn. Before I could interject, he added, "Cereal does not count as a meal." Turning to Marcus, he said, "I'll let you eat in peace, but don't think I don't want every single detail of what you're up to before the night is over." With that, he walked away, greeting another customer who was sitting down at the bar.

"He means it too. He's relentless sometimes." I took a bite of the meat pie. It was heaven. He had been right: somehow, I had skipped lunch again today. We sat in silence as the pies were quickly consumed; apparently, I wasn't the only one neglecting my stomach.

"So, how about you tell me what you're doing here," I said. "I would think the council has better things to do than deal with a strange but not really illegal head situation in rural Ontario."

"You'd be right in that assessment." Marcus sat up, donning his serious expression again. He reached into his pocket and pulled out a metal disc, placing it on the table. Holding his hand over it seemed to cause a small glyph to illuminate the table. I leaned over to take a closer look. A privacy charm? I'd never seen one of these before, though I'd heard of them. They were used to conceal private conversations without making it look like you were. Anyone else listening in would hear us chatting about something uninteresting, like the weather. Marcus had all sorts of interesting toys; I was a tad jealous. Working for MCIB seemed to have some fascinating perks.

Marcus waited until the charm was fully activated before continuing.

"Normally, I wouldn't be sent to a situation like this. However, the sample that Alrick sent us had traces of a new compound that has been identified in several other investigations in London. This is the first time it's been identified in North America." He paused, taking a sip of the beer. "The compound has some unique properties that are worrying the council. I've been sent to track down the source and identify the manufacturer."

I digested that for a moment. "Unique properties?" I asked. "If it's enough to worry the council, it must be something interesting."

He looked at me, all the earlier humour gone from his expression. "Interesting isn't the word I would use. The compound makes magical creatures mortal." He let that bombshell hit home before continuing on. "When I say the council is worried, it would be more accurate to say they are extremely alarmed, bordering on panic."

I leaned back. Holy shit. That had massive implications. Many magical creatures were essentially immortal. If a drug out there could make them mortal, the balance of power in our world could be completely undone. This was no small thing. More alarmingly, how did it end up in a head on my lawn? This investigation had gone from strange to "intensely scary end of the world as we know it", very fast.

Chapter 5

If the world was potentially going to be torn apart by a sinister drug that nullified magic, I would need another beer. Or several. I waved at Brandon, asking for another round.

Brandon dropped off the beers at the table without comment. I looked up for the first time since we had started talking, finally noticing the noise of people talking; the pub was getting busy. Creemore came out at night and, more often than not, showed up at the Meet at some point in the evening. Tonight was no exception. Tuesdays were open mic nights, and from the looks of it, things were about to get started. Usually, I would stay and enjoy the music, but Marcus's news had effectively killed my earlier relaxed state. I felt more like going home and losing myself in a book with a less stressful reality than my current one.

Suddenly eager to get home, I glanced at Marcus. He seemed to be lost in his own thoughts as well. "Where are you staying tonight?" I asked, breaking the spell of concentration that had come over us both.

Marcus shrugged, as if the thought of sleeping was irrelevant to him.

"There's a great B&B up the road. I can show you if you

want. It's between ski season and beach season, so it won't be that busy," I offered.

"It's fine, really, I was going to sleep in my car," he said, as if that wasn't an unusual thing to say. He turned the charm off and slipped it back in his pocket, understanding that we were done talking for the night.

"What? Why?" I asked, shocked at his casual statement. Why would anyone sleep in a car when there was a perfectly suitable alternative? I had slept in some really unpleasant circumstances during my time in the service. I was a prominent advocate of comfortable beds when available.

He gave me a regarding look. "You may not have noticed, but I am soulless," he said, as if this somehow explained his prejudice against comfortable sleeping conditions. Seeing my continued confusion, he continued. "Most hotels or inns see the soulless as, at best, a liability, at worst, a monster that will rip off the heads of the other guests and eat their still-beating hearts."

Well, that was a somewhat specific and graphic description of a worst-case scenario. I would have hazarded a guess that this may have been something that had actually happened. Marcus shrugged again. "The soulless don't have a great history. While most of us are indeed dangerous, we are most of the time very well contained, but it only takes one person to ruin it for the rest of us." He rubbed his face tiredly. "The current political state of affairs in America has just exacerbated the situation."

I wanted to be shocked at this admission, but I wasn't. I had similar thoughts of the Soulless when Marcus first appeared in my driveway earlier today. Over the past decade, anti-magical sentiment had grown in both size and political power. The soulless, being some of the more dangerous among our kind, must have been bearing the brunt of the human movement to segregate and control the magical population. I wanted to believe that Creemore, given its odd magical population, would be exempt from these prejudices. Still, I wasn't confident that was the case. In a surge of righteous anger at the unfairness of it, and to appease some of my guilt at having had similar thoughts about him, I made an impulse decision. I hoped I wouldn't regret it later.

"Well, that's not happening. You can use one of the empty rooms in the house." I carried on before he could say anything. "Besides, it will be easier to work together to track the source of the demon if we're in the same location."

Marcus looked at me for a long while. I was getting uncomfortable with his intense inspection of my face when he finally nodded. "That will work, thank you," he said.

"Good, well, that's settled, then. We can come up with a plan for tomorrow in the morning. I don't know about you, but it's been a long day," I said, standing up and grabbing my jacket and keys. Looking to see if I could escape Brandon's earlier threatened interrogation, I saw him distracted at the bar and hurried toward the door, with Marcus close behind me.

Breathing in the fresh spring air outside the pub, I headed for my truck, too tired to notice Marcus watching me intently before making his way over toward the SUV. The drive home was only about twenty minutes, but it felt much longer.

Marcus beat me to the house. I found him leaning against the SUV, holding a black duffle bag. With the crescent moon casting a ghostly light over him, he looked like a shadowy apparition of vengeance. He fell into step beside me as I headed toward the porch. I froze. In my exhaustion, I had overlooked the implications of him being in the house. Kit was in there. Shit.

"What?" he asked, sensing my unease. When I didn't answer right away, he sighed. "Look, it's fine. I don't need to come in if you're worried. I'm more of a chicken-eating kind of man than a beating hearts sort, but I can understand your hesitancy."

I laughed dryly. "I'll admit I am concerned about your presence in my home. Not because of what you are, more that you work for the MCIB. I may or may not have some less than legal occupants." I paused, trying to phrase this properly, so I didn't sound like an insane person. "But look, we can work around this. Pinky swear you will not report or hurt anyone in this house, and we'll be all good." Yes. That didn't sound crazy or childish at all. I was too tired to come up with something better. Stress and social situations fried my brain. Despite having just met Marcus, he struck me as the type who would abide by a promise made. My instincts had rarely led me astray.

"A pinky swear?" he said, clearly trying to decide if I had lost my mind. "Are you five?"

"I was once, and the habit stuck. Why change what works?" I shrugged.

He looked tired, clearly defeated by my crazy logic. Obviously, my plan was brilliant.

"Okay, look, I'm tired, you're tired. If you can tell me your not-quite-legal occupant is not a danger to themselves or others, I will agree to this ridiculous token promise if it will let me find a bed faster," he said.

"They are not," I said, relieved that he had agreed so quickly. I held out my pinky.

"You have got to be kidding me. You're serious?" Marcus

looked at my outstretched hand like it was a snake.

"Yes," I said solemnly. Pinky swears were a serious business.

He held out his hand while shaking his head. Clearly, my credibility was taking a hit here, but I believed you needed to follow through with these things. As Marcus hooked his hand with mine, I felt a zing of electricity pass between us. While my brain understood he was a dangerous MCIB agent, the rest of my body didn't seem to care. My cheeks heated, and I pulled away awkwardly and turned to go into the house, glad of the darkness to hide my blush.

"Come on, let's get you settled," I said, trying not to sound as shaken as I felt. I led him to the second floor of the house, where the small guest suites were located. Kit and I lived up in the converted attic space. Our small apartment had two bedrooms, a small sitting room, and a bathroom. The suites on the second floor were the first thing I had tackled when we arrived. Each had a self-contained bathroom and bedroom. I kept them clean and freshly stocked, hoping someone would magically appear and rent them. While Marcus wasn't what I was expecting, I was glad to have a place for him. I led him to the room at the end of the long hall, furthest away from Abby.

"Okay, this is you," I said, opening the door for him. "There are towels in the bathroom. If you need anything, I'm down the hall and up the stairs," I said.

Marcus nodded. "Thank you, it looks wonderful, much better than the car," he smiled tiredly.

"Okay, cool. Well, sleep well, we can talk in the morning, I guess." I turned abruptly and escaped down the hall toward my room before he could say anything else.

Smooth, yes, I was so smooth, not awkward at all. Marcus threw me in a way I didn't understand. He was attractive, and

I was no nun. I could appreciate an excellent male specimen. Perhaps it was because the only date I had been on was well over a year ago, and I didn't even recall his name. Yes, that must be it. Opening the door to the attic, I stepped into the small sitting room of the apartment.

"Kit?" I called out, hoping she was already asleep. I wanted to let her know about our new guest in case she was up doing fox things in the middle of the night. After a few moments, I heard her claws on the hardwood floors coming toward me. "Hey, there you are," I said, scooping her up and scratching her ears. "We have a new guest. It's the MCIB agent I told you about earlier." She looked at me, alarmed. "No, no, don't panic. I think it's okay. I made him pinky swear not to report you."

Kit looked at me like I was an idiot.

"Look, it's not perfect, but I will keep you safe, and I've got to know him a bit tonight. I don't think he would hurt you, okay? Can you trust me on this?" Kit didn't look convinced, but she nodded anyway before hopping down and heading back toward the bedroom. I followed behind, leaving a wake of clothing behind me. Digging out an old T-shirt from a drawer, I collapsed on the bed beside her. I fired off a quick text to Abby, letting her know there was someone new in the house before tossing the phone on the bedside table. Man, what a day. I rolled over to look at Kit, who had perched sleepily on a pillow. Yawning, she turned around, flicking me with her tail. "Thanks! Love you too," I said, rolling over. I stared at the water stain on my ceiling. Suddenly, it didn't seem like such a big problem anymore. Before I could think more about the dramatic shift in my perspective, I fell into a deep sleep.

Chapter 6

A terrifying screeching coming from the sitting room jarred me violently out of sleep. "Shit," I said, jumping from the bed and scrambling toward the sound. I came to a halt in the middle of the room, trying to pinpoint the location of the sound. It was coming from under the sofa. I sat down beside it, trying to calm my racing heart. Kit had night terrors. I knew I couldn't wake her up—I had tried before and just ended up getting bitten and scratched—but I could be here for her when she woke up. Her terrified cries permeated the darkness, breaking my heart. Just as I thought she was coming back to consciousness, the door to the apartment burst open. Framed in the doorway was a beast bathed in red shadows, brandishing a broadsword engulfed in flames. Marcus looked like an avenging angel come to render judgement on the evil that dared threaten us. Shocked but too tired to react, I stared at him in the doorway.

Marcus finally seemed to notice the tableau of me sitting on the floor, looking unhappy but not under threat. I shook my head in response to the question in his eyes. The sounds had faded to whimpering. Slowly, Kit nosed her way out from under the sofa and crawled into my lap, unaware of our audience. I covered her with a blanket and whispered calm nonsense words at her until she seemed to settle.

Marcus let his magic fade from his skin. I looked up, taking in the full view of him. He seemed to have skipped getting dressed in his rush to protect us from whatever threat he thought was in here. I took in the sight of his hard body in the moonlight, clothed only in boxer briefs, and his long, powerful legs. My eyes worked their way up to his smooth chest that I itched to touch. This image of him, sword in hand in nothing but underwear, was going to haunt my dreams. I was sure of it.

Marcus leaned the sword up against the door frame and walked toward us tentatively. "It's a shifter?" he asked gently, understanding that whatever was going on, the tiny creature in my lap was terrified. Stopping a few feet away, he crouched on the floor, looking at me for clarification.

"This is Kit. She had a night terror," I offered by way of explanation.

"I see. I'll leave you to settle her. I'd rather not frighten her more. Call me if you require anything," he said awkwardly as he stood and left silently through the open door. I let out the breath I hadn't known I was holding. I was glad I didn't have to explain or ask him to leave.

He was right. He would frighten her more by being there. Sometimes the best kind of help was the sort that knew when to give the space required. I looked down at Kit. I had been stroking her back absently, which had lulled her back into a deep sleep. She never really woke up after a night terror, and from what I could tell, she didn't recall them the next day. I sighed and scooped up the little bundle of blankets and fur, carrying her back to her bed. I had gotten her the toddler-style bed, with its silly blue paint and silver stars, hoping to reclaim some of my pillows and blankets during the winter. Most nights it worked, too. I placed her on the bed, glad that she didn't wake. Leaning over to my bedside table, I grabbed the baby monitor out of the drawer and turned it on. I would not sleep again tonight. I might as well head downstairs and get a start on the pile of paperwork Alrick had emailed me earlier. Shrugging on a sweater that smelled mostly clean and some warmer pyjama pants, I picked up the handheld monitor and went in search of my laptop and some strong coffee.

Arriving in the kitchen, I didn't bother to turn the light on. The bright moonlight cast deep shadows around the kitchen, but it was light enough to see my destination. I headed for the coffee machine while dumping my laptop on the kitchen island. Turning the machine on, I perched on a stool to wait for the brew to finish. I hated nights like this, the ones that felt like the world was sleeping peacefully, and I was the only one awake. What was worse, I had been here before on countless nights. It was starting to feel like I was living the same day repeatedly, like a terrible movie. Kit and I were not really progressing forward, prisoners of the horrors we had witnessed, and too scared to look beyond our self-made cages to the future. This had to stop—it was wearing me down slowly but surely—but I didn't know where to start. I put my head in my hands and leaned my arms on the countertop as I was flooded with all the choices I had made to bring us here. The doubt was overwhelming. Had I done the right thing with Kit–or myself? Guilt, uncertainty, and anger ate at my mind until there was nothing left but a screaming wind of misery howling through my brain.

Someone pushed a mug of coffee in front of me, derailing the out-of-control crazy train I was on. I took a shuddering breath and looked up to see Marcus standing in the middle of the dark kitchen, sipping a coffee and looking at me with concern written on his dark face. I took the warm mug between my hands, trying to school my face to look like I had it together when clearly I did not. "Thanks," I said, nodding to the coffee.

"Can I assume that the small fox shifter is the subject of our pinky swear?" he said as he settled onto the stool opposite me. I didn't really want to talk about this right now, but I felt like I owed him some sort of explanation. He had, after all, busted in to save us.

"Yes, she is," I said, trying to find the words to condense this story down to the facts so my raw heart wouldn't have to relive the emotions attached to it. "She was traumatized when her village was flattened in the war. She can no longer shift," I blurted. That about covered the essential details. I hoped he didn't want to know more, suddenly feeling exhausted.

"I see," he said, understanding dawning. "Shifter law is very specific about situations such as this," he said seriously.

I looked at him, panicking. Was he going to go back on his promise? I didn't like where this was going. "She's a child!" I cried angrily. No way was this man going to take Kit to the shifters. I wouldn't let that happen.

Marcus sighed, taking a sip of his coffee. "I've come to understand that pinky swears are a serious vow, one I have no intention of breaking, so maybe put your magic away and drink your coffee."

I looked down at my hands, which were glowing green. It was rare for me to lose control like that. I wasn't even sure what I would have done with it. Would I grow a scary-looking houseplant or something? My magic wasn't great for much beyond potions and tending the garden. I turned my mind inwards and reeled in my magic, settling it down to the still pond of power within me.

"Sorry," I said, and I meant it. I wasn't used to people knowing our secrets, and the feeling was disconcerting. That was clearly a Me problem. There was no reason to take it out on Marcus.

Marcus stood up. "Do you mind if I light a fire? I may be part vampire, but even Canada's springs are too cold for me." I looked at him, grateful that he had dropped the subject without follow-up.

"Sure," I said, picking up my laptop and coffee as I led him into the large sitting room. This part of the house was what I first fell in love with. Its deep stone fireplace with a heavy wood mantle and the deep green walls with rich raw wood wainscoting made the entire room feel like a wealthy country estate in Scotland. It was totally out of place with the rest of the house, but I would never change it. I sat down on the dark brown sofa, sinking into its plush softness. The matching sofas had come with the house and were in surprisingly good condition.

Marcus crouched in front of the fireplace and held out his hand over the pile of logs. His magic briefly danced on the surface of his skin before igniting the kindling. Flames licked up along the logs.

"Neat trick," I said, wrapping a blanket around my shoulders and opening my laptop.

"I would make an excellent boy scout," he said, taking the place on the sofa across from me. I skimmed through my email without really reading anything. Giving up, I closed the screen and placed it on the old oak coffee table in front of me. Looking across at Marcus, I saw he was watching me intently again.

I sighed, picking up my coffee from the table and settling deeper into the soft cushions. "Can I ask you something?"

Marcus smiled. "I believe you just did."

I rolled my eyes. For someone so serious, he sure did have a smart mouth. I liked it. "Why MCIB? Is that not an unconventional choice for a bound soulless?" I asked.

"You mean why am I not an assassin, villain, or mercenary going around chopping people's heads off? Or being wantonly violent for the highest bidder, like others of my kind?" he shot back at me.

"Yes. That." I said, too late to backtrack on the question now that it was out there. Might as well own it and face it head-on. Clearly, I had hit a nerve with this line of questioning, though it wasn't my intent.

Marcus put his mug on the coffee table in front of him before leaning back and stretching his long legs out in front of him. On anyone else, it would have looked relaxing. With him, it just looked like a powerful jungle cat coiling its energy, ready to pounce on its prey. He sighed, the tension seeming to go out from him. "It's a touchy subject for me. I am on the more unusual end of the behaviour spectrum when it comes to the Soulless. I find it exhausting to constantly be trying to convince people that just because I can kill doesn't mean I do so mindlessly." He paused before staring at me intensely. "You have killed," he said matter-of-factly. "Imagine if that was the only thing that defined your existence for others." He let that sink in for a moment. "I joined MCIB for selfish reasons. I think I was looking for some noble purpose while satisfying my need to be the modern-day Sherlock. I like mysteries. The stranger the better while working within a system that, while not perfect, does some good despite the astronomical amount of paperwork." After a moment, he asked, "Why did you join the army?"

I laughed. "Nothing so interesting as you. They offered to pay my university fees. I think, in actuality, I was a diversity hire. The military is mostly made up of humans. With the ongoing tensions and the newly signed Inclusion Act, they were looking to increase their magical population numbers."

The Inclusion Act had been signed, hoping to bring the two societies together. However, it seemed to have had the opposite effect. Human governmental agencies were obligated to employ magic users; magical governmental agencies like the Magic Council and MCIB were not required to reciprocate. This had bred more than a little resentment from both the human population and larger human government agencies, and unrest and anger had festered as a result. Recently, it had escalated to bombing and other kinds of attacks on the magical communities.

I snorted in disgust. "They must have looked at me like they had won the lottery, being both female and a witch." I shrugged. "It worked out okay. They paid for both my undergrad and master's degrees for the low price of my sanity and part of my soul. No big deal."

"Do you regret it?" he questioned.

"No. Maybe. Sometimes, but mostly not. I was younger than and naively optimistic that I would see the world while being the heroic peacekeeper in faraway lands. That vision imploded after my first tour, but I stuck with it, still hoping to I don't know, really. It was all I knew by so I stayed, sinking deeper into the muddy waters of Special Projects," I said darkly, "until something more important pulled me away."

"Kit?" he prodded

Ah, we were circling back to this again. "Yes, Kit. That is a decision I absolutely don't regret, though looking back, I think I was ready to leave by then, anyway." I hoped that was the end of his questions. Seeming to sense my reluctance to continue on this topic, he picked up his mug and headed to the kitchen.

"Refill?" he asked, holding out his hand for my cup. Somehow, the small courtesy felt more like an invitation to something more than a fresh coffee. He looked down at me with hunger in his eyes, like he wanted to make me forget my pain for a little while. I was momentarily pleased the attraction I was feeling wasn't one-sided. As tempting as he was, bathed in firelight, looking every inch the noble warrior while the smell of wood smoke soothed my soul, I couldn't move past my mistrust of him even for one night.

"No, thank you," I said, declining more than just coffee. I stared at my hands, unable to look at him. When I finally lifted my gaze, he had disappeared into the kitchen. I pulled the blanket tight around me and settled my head onto the nearby throw pillow. Watching the fire crackle happily, letting it pacify my worry, I slowly drifted off to sleep.

Chapter 7

I woke up slowly to the sun shining through the big bay window. The sounds of a lively debate were coming from the kitchen. Slowly, I stretched out the residual aches from sleeping awkwardly on the sofa. I sat up, throwing off the blanket. It was time to face the day. Heading to the kitchen, my nose seemed to have died and gone to heaven. Marcus manned the stove, surrounded by evidence of having already churned out several rounds of pancakes. Shock at finding an MCIB agent making pancakes in my kitchen while laughing with Abby gave over quickly to the grumbling of my empty stomach. Whatever alternate reality I had stumbled upon smelled fantastic and, given the number of dishes already accumulating on the counter, I was late to the party. Abby sat at the kitchen island drinking her coffee and clearly waiting for the next instalment. I refilled my coffee mug from the night before and joined her.

Abby looked me over with a critical eye. "You look like shit, but whatever. Here, explain this thing to Marcus," she said, waving her hands toward the milk on the counter. "He doesn't believe me it's weird."

I had no idea what she was talking about. I looked at her and then at the milk. "You sure it's not you who's weird? Dare

I say even crazy?"

Marcus chuffed out a laugh without taking his attention away from his pan. "That's what I said," he retorted, tossing a pancake onto a plate and setting it in front of me. He smiled at me before winking and turning back to the stovetop. Who was this charming chef in my kitchen? What had he done with serious Mr Agent Marcus? I looked at the pancake suspiciously before digging in. If Abby had survived the pancakes, I was probably safe.

Abby glared at me. "Look, your milk is in a freaking *bag*!" she said, pointing at it like it was an alien that had just landed in front of her. "I've travelled all over this world and several others. No one puts milk in bags. It's bizarre," I groaned inwardly. Abby had been railing on this for nearly three years. This obsession of hers was not healthy.

Marcus brought his own pancakes over to join us. Sitting down, he looked at Abby with an earnest expression. "It's perfectly practical, not weird at all." I took a bite of the pancake, trying to hide my smile. He was winding her up, and I was just going to sit here and enjoy the show. I missed this. For the last few years, it had just been the three of us here, and it had been quiet. I missed the noise and laughter of people. I ate my pancake silently, watching the two of them bicker about the merits of bagged milk when Kit skittered into the kitchen and hopped up on my lap.

"Morning, Kit," I said, rubbing between her ears. It seemed like the drama of last night had been forgotten. Relief flooded me. Marcus raised an eyebrow in question, and I shook my head. No need to worry, it seemed. Kit looked at my plate and then up at me. "Want some?" I asked. As if taking my question as permission, she snatched the remainder of my breakfast off my plate and hopped over the counter to land perfectly on top of the fridge. She clutched her stolen goods in her little white paws with a pleased expression on her face. "Hey! Thief!" I said, shaking my fist. Kit smirked at me. Clearly, stolen breakfast tasted better.

Marcus and Abby had stopped their argument in favour of watching me be robbed of my delicious pancakes. Marcus dropped one of his on my plate without comment. I took a bite angrily while scowling at Kit's smug little face.

"So what's the plan, Scooby Crew?" Abby asked, "I'm not working today, so I can help if you need it." Abby worked part time at the bookstore in the village, though I suspected it was more for the gossip than an actual need for employment.

"Scooby Crew?" Marcus shot Abby an unimpressed look.

"Sherlock?" she asked in a follow-up. I wondered when the two of them had become chummy. How long had I been asleep?

"Better," he said, chuckling. Turning to me, he pulled his serious work face back on. "I have a locating charm to find the rest of the demon remains if they're still here somewhere. I'd like you to scry the area to narrow the search area. The charm only has a range of about half a mile."

Scrying was a pretty essential skill for most witches. I was out of practice, but it wouldn't be too hard to pull that off.

"Sure, I can do that," I said, finishing my pancakes. "Let me get cleaned up and gather my supplies. Shouldn't take too long." Marcus nodded in agreement. Pushing back from the counter, I headed up the stairs to shower. Behind me, I heard Kit's tiny claws click on the steps. I waited for her before going into our apartment. Crouching down, I looked at her closely to see any lingering effects from the night before. I couldn't tell, but she seemed okay. Sometimes, her inability to speak was frustrating. Walking through the sitting room, I chucked my dirty clothes in the general direction of the laundry hamper and headed for the shower.

Dressing quickly, I donned an old T-shirt and jeans that were thankfully not covered in paint. I threw my long hair back in a messy braid, forgoing makeup. I had never been keen on the rituals of getting pretty. I think it had something to do with my propensity for getting dirty; makeup would just be more gunk to wash off at the end of the day. I headed toward the haphazard storage room on the second floor, where I had stored all my old magical supplies. The floor-to-ceiling shelves and tall windows led me to think the room had once been a library; now a mix of boxes, crates and renovation supplies, it was disorganized mayhem.

Shoving some old crates out of the way, I finally located my trunk from my parents' house. I hadn't really settled anywhere in the years since leaving home. When I had eventually bought this house, my mum had leapt at the opportunity to unload all the various boxes and crates I had stored in her basement. I still hadn't made an effort to go through any of them.

I was hoping all my magical supplies were still in here from when I was still in high school. I had gone to a mixed school as a teenager, which meant my magical education was lacking, but I had taken the basics. Mixed schools were a noble effort to end segregation between humans and magic users. They taught both magical basics and the typical human curriculum.

They don't have integrated schools anymore; there was just too much risk and animosity. It was also to keep humans safe from creatures just coming into their powers during adolescence. Like with most things in the teenage years, it was an unstable time in terms of both control and strength. Sometimes I wondered if there would ever be a world where the two societies would reach a place of peace. Pushing the heavy thoughts away, I dug through the trunk. My hand landed on a small box that rattled promisingly. I opened it up to find a few scry crystals; plucking them out of the case, I headed back down the stairs. I was going to need something from the demon for the spell to work. Given that my friend was ash, that might be tricky.

Arriving in the now empty kitchen, I headed for the back door that led to the garden. I loved my garden. It was the one place I didn't feel like a failed witch. I excelled at growing all sorts of things and coveted my rare plants like a dragon hoarded gold. All of my trips to the local fae market nearby had been in pursuit of some plant or another. I had amassed quite the collection over the past three years and drank in the sights and scents as I passed through the garden to the dilapidated shed tucked into the side of the house. Opening the bucket full of ash, I tried not to breathe. Oh shit, it smelled like regurgitated roadkill. I struggled to hold back the gag I desperately wanted to let go of. Looking around the shelves above me, I found some electrical tape on a shelf and quickly stuck some ash on it, wrapping it around the crystal. It looked like a child's art project, but I was reasonably confident it would work.

Heading back inside, I joined Abby and Marcus at the kitchen island. Marcus had produced an old paper map from somewhere, laying it out on the bright stone counter.

Abby snickered at my locating crystal. "It's so pretty."

I humphed at her while feeding my power slowly down the string holding the crystal. The whole concoction glowed a dim green and started to move.

The crystal circled above the map for a few moments before its elliptical changed unnaturally and then dropped suddenly into the map atop Miller's Dairy Farm.

"Ha! It's ugly, but it worked!" I said in triumph, which was instantaneously deflated when I noticed where we were headed. "Well, damn."

Abby laughed. "Well, that's me out." She took her coffee and headed out the back door to the garden. "Good luck!" she shot over her shoulder. "You're gonna need it! It's Wednesday!" she cackled, even harder, as she disappeared into the garden.

Marcus looked at me, confused. "This is going to require some explanation."

I sighed, sitting down heavily on the kitchen stool. "It's Miller's Dairy Farm," I said, as if somehow that explained everything. The dairy farm wasn't really the problem.

I looked over at the calendar on the fridge. Abby was right. It was Wednesday. "Double shit," I said, mostly to myself, slumping back on the stool. Nothing could ever just be easy, could it?

Chapter 8

"I still have several follow-up questions on your vague and unhelpful statement," he said, not looking overly impressed with my previous answers.

I wondered where to start. "Well, the dairy isn't really a problem. About half a mile from the dairy is a portal to the fae realm. Which makes it a place we would generally like to avoid. The enchantments protecting the portal have a habit of luring unsuspecting people in when they get too close. Then they just sort of end up disappearing." I shrugged.

I tried not to think too hard about what that meant. "If that doesn't work, spitting unfriendly creatures out to eat you is also an option for deterring unwanted guests." I took a deep breath because it wasn't just the portal and its many charms that were an issue today.

"Normally, it's just citizens of Fae that travel through that area, but once a week on Wednesdays there's a market of sorts. Though I use the term market here loosely, very loosely." It was more a place to buy and sell magic items that were not particularly legal. There were also random interspecies orgies in bushes and vendors that wouldn't take no for an answer, but would be happy to take an arm. Market-going creatures had been known to kidnap humans who strayed inside the boundaries, which wasn't ideal since we looked very human and thus very kidnappable. The entire event started at dawn and went on until dusk, like a magic-fuelled rave with shops. If you were not of the Fae, it was not a place you wanted to go without a compelling reason. It was thankfully quarantined by barrier wards set by the local coven, who had decreed the event a public safety issue, but once inside the boundaries, you were on your own.

Marcus looked relieved. "A fae market shouldn't be too much of a problem for us," he said with more certainty than I felt.

Oh, to be blessed with the confidence of the ignorant. I shook my head. I had been to the market a handful of times to find hard to get ingredients or plants for some of my potions. I had always sworn every time that I would never go back again. Last time, I had stumbled upon a faun and gwyllion having fun together—things I can never unsee. I didn't even know how they made the anatomy of all the various appendages and orifices fit together.

Resigned to my fate, I nodded at Marcus. "Okay, well, let's get going then".

The dairy wasn't far, but it was impossible to know how long the walk to the gate would be. The magic barrier could make it take a few minutes or a few hours. I headed to our makeshift mud room to pack up some supplies. I didn't want to walk into the market unprepared. You only make that mistake once. I shrugged on an extra-large flannel work jacket, an old floppy hat, and rubber boots that came up nearly to my knees, tucking my jeans into them. I looked like a deranged fisherman zombie. It was perfect. Heaving on my heavy backpack, I clomped back to the kitchen to find some lunch and extra water. As a rule, I avoided eating fae food. Even outside the realm of the Fae, there could be some bizarre side effects.

Marcus stood by the door, looking impatient while he fiddled on his phone. He was dressed in black slacks, dress shoes, and a casual black wool sweater. He looked every inch the MCIB agent. The only thing out of place was his broadsword that was strapped to his back.

He looked up from his phone, taking in my outfit. "What?" I asked, daring him to say something.

"Nothing. I have absolutely nothing to say," he grinned at me.

"Oh, that's fine, laugh it up, buddy, but don't come crying to me when you ruin your expensive-looking outfit." Walking past him toward my truck, I tossed my sack in the back and climbed in. Marcus followed me, sliding into the passenger seat. I looked at him as my eyebrows crept up. I had expected him to take his own car. Well, I shouldn't be questioning my luck at the lack of argument. Turning the engine over, I headed down the driveway and pulled onto the road leading to the dairy. We drove in silence while Marcus made displeased faces at his phone.

Curiosity finally made me ask, "Is something wrong?" Marcus looked up, clearly distracted by whatever he was reading.

"Wrong? Yes, but not relevant to this investigation, I don't think. Before being sent here, I was part of the Anti-Magic Terrorism Task Force. We were working toward tracking terrorist groups online. It seems all the chatter we'd been tracking has gone suddenly silent." He sat back, looking thoughtful. I had nothing to add to that. Watching the escalating protests and anti-magic rhetoric on TV was much different than having the reality of it in the passenger seat of your truck. We drove the rest of the way, both lost in our own thoughts.

Pulling off to the side of the road, I announced, "We're here," and got out of the pickup. I hauled my backpack out of the truck bed. "Ready?"

"Yep, lead the way," he said.

We started down the path. About half a mile in, I felt the first ward barrier wash over us. This one was to conceal the location from unsuspecting humans. We carried on as the sun rose overhead. It was getting warm, so I took off my jacket, wrapping it around my waist.

Marcus whispered in my ear, "It's much harder to admire your ass when you're covering it up like that." His closeness made me jump. The sneaky bastard. I turned around to face him. "Are you flirting with me? Isn't that unprofessional?" I asked in mock seriousness. I enjoyed his playful attitude; he seemed to have relaxed since yesterday, letting all of his business exterior fade.

He considered me for a moment before grinning. "Absolutely and probably," he answered. "I've never been good at passing up a tempting opportunity, nor at being very professional for long periods of time. I find it very taxing on my sensibilities." He leaned toward me as my heart thumped wildly. "You are very tempting," he purred in my ear, sending shivers down my spine.

I laughed at him, spinning around, and started walking down the path again. I was unsure what to make of that. Marcus was so straightforward that it threw me off guard. I'd be lying if I said he wasn't tempting, too. His forthright manner turned me on, and he was easy to look at, to say the least. It was hard to ignore someone who just put their desire out there unapologetically.

We carried on, both lost in our own thoughts, for nearly an hour. I was regretting not bringing sunscreen. My fair skin was burning in the scorching sun. I would be waking up tomorrow with more freckles, for sure. I faced the unpleasant choice between being too hot in my jacket or burning to a crisp. Before I was forced to cover up, we finally approached the second barrier. I paused.

"This one stings a bit," I said in warning. Marcus shrugged and slipped through, unaffected. Show-off. I hurried through, trying to ignore the lighting-like zap the barrier gave me. Once through, I took in the sights and noisy din of the market. It was just as colourful and strange as I remembered. Stalls jammed the grove of trees that served as the central area.

Colourful banners in languages I couldn't read hung from branches. While we looked on, several rock trolls crossed the path, manoeuvring their large stone bodies around us, looking annoyed and shouting in our general direction what I gather were insults. We moved off the noisy main pathway and into a more secluded thicket of trees, where Marcus fished out the locating charm from his pocket. It looked like a small stone compass. He held his hand over the charm, saying a few words to activate it. It glowed red, and the small arrow spun before finally pointing in the direction of the lake. We worked through the press of bodies in the central portion of the market, following the path indicated by the charm. I couldn't help but peruse the wares displayed on the stalls, hoping to see some plants I had been hoping to find—no reason I couldn't find a dead body and shop at the same time.

"Demons first, then we can window shop," Marcus said, as if reading my mind. We picked up the pace and left the noisy mess of creatures behind, travelling down a quiet trail that led through the trees and opened onto the blue-green lake. In the distance, I could see the fae portal shimmering in the sunlight.

"This way." Marcus pointed toward the water.

As we approached the lake, a noise I hadn't noticed before now seemed to grow louder: I could make out high-pitched squeals and manic laughter.

"Ah, shit," I moaned. I knew this had been too easy so far. Nothing had stepped on us or tried to eat us yet.

"What?" Marcus asked, concerned.

I pointed to a spot on the shores of the lake where the water rose up like waves, dancing along the surface before crashing down upon small laughing creatures. "Those are water sprites. Tell me we aren't going that way," I said. "Okay, I won't," he said, as he strode right toward them, watching the charm arrow spin. It was very tempting to let this play out.

Clearly, Marcus had no idea what a pain the ass water sprites were. Sometimes the best education comes from hands-on experience. I didn't hurry as I followed him, not wanting to get close to what I assumed would be a wet and messy encounter. Standing a few feet away, I watched Marcus follow the charm's direction until he reached the edge of the lake where the sprites were playing. They stopped their game to watch him. Here we go. With no warning, the group leapt from the water and snatched wildly at Marcus, their tiny green hands tugging at his ears and hair. One had climbed under his shirt. I laughed as he tried to collar and throw them off. Mostly, the tiny fairies were like overgrown mosquitoes with a twisted sense of humour. I had run afoul of them last year and lost a good chunk of hair for my troubles.

Marcus called up his magic and released a burst of heat from his skin, powerful enough that the sprites jumped off him for the cool safety of the water. Chittering angrily, they threw globs of mud and weeds at him. So distracted I was by the entertainment in front of me, I hadn't noticed a few stray sprites sneak up beside me, grabbing at my backpack and throwing me off balance. The tiny creatures laughed at my sudden alarm as they dragged me to the water's edge and pulled me into the muddy water. One of them lifted a small log as if to hit me with it. Stronger than they looked, the log came down beside me, narrowly missing my face. Seeing that the sprite had lost its weapon, I picked it up, hoping to turn the tables on them. My fingers sank into the flesh of the wood that clearly wasn't wood at all. It was an arm. Oh, so gross! I dropped it back in the water.

I guess we had found the rest of the body.

Having had more than enough of the sprites' nonsense, I called up my magic and flung it wildly at them. It was just light, so it wouldn't actually do anything, but they didn't know that. Seeing that both Marcus and I were willing to fry them with magic, the sprites hightailed it deeper into the lake, making several rude gestures before diving under the water.

A mud-covered Marcus walked over to me, helping me out of the muck. He had a few bite marks on his face and probably needed a shower, but looked otherwise unscathed.

"Well, that was fun," he said, grinning, as if being attacked by tiny, vicious sprites had been a laugh a minute. He was certifiably nuts.

"You don't get out much, do you?" I said, glaring at his crazy grin.

"No, not really." Picking up the half-rotted arm, I promised myself there would be several long showers and sanitizer baths in my future. I tossed it on the grass next to Marcus.

"It looks like we found our missing body."

Chapter 9

We hauled as many of the body parts onto the grass that we could find in the shallow water. It was slimy, dirty work. After a while, the pile looked to be everything minus a head. Marcus wiped his hands on his pants and pulled off the charm he had used on the head the day before. It flashed blue once again, and the rest of the body turned to ash.

"This is our demon—he had similar demon marks on his arms. But the magic reads as mortal," he said.

Sifting through the ash of the former demon, we found a few scraps of paper with illegible writing but no wallet or other identification. I guess it would have been a stretch to have a demon carry a convenient driver's licence or copy of the master evil plan. I shoved more of the ash with my foot when it hit something with a thud. Digging through goop, I pulled out an old cell phone. Muddy and wet, it looked like it had seen better days. Muddy and wet, it looked like it had seen better days, but it could be the answer to our problem.

"Look what I found," I said, holding up my prize.

"That may be of use if we can retrieve the data." Marcus looked pleased. I handed it to him, and he dropped it into the plastic bag with the other small clues we had collected.

"I'll have to get it back to London for our techs to take a look. We should probably head back now. I should get going as soon as possible. Let's leave the ashes. They'll wash away in the next rain." He slogged his way through the mud up onto the grass, unsuccessfully trying to wipe away the mud from his now ruined shoes.

I followed him up the steep bank, glad of my rubber boots. "I may know a guy," I said casually.

"A guy?" Marcus looked at me sceptically.

"Yes, a guy," I said confidently, "he's a former military special analyst, which is essentially a government-sanctioned hacker. He's private security now, but he may be able to help us, and he's local."

Marcus considered it for a moment. "Sure. I'd rather not wait too long to see if anything is retrievable off here, in case the trail goes cold. I'm willing to bend the rules a bit." He headed out toward the path that had led us here.

I had just moved to follow him when a long vine shot up from the surface of the water and tightly wrapped around me, yanking me into the lake. I yelled in surprise before the sound was cut off by the water closing over my head. I kicked at the lake bed, trying to find some purchase to push up to the surface while trying to free my arms from the vice-like grip of the vines that were squeezing me tighter the more I struggled.

My lungs were burning. I needed to get free before I passed out. I called up my magic, feeding it to the vines, hoping to take control of them. My magic was clashing with the magic of the plant, but I finally broke the connection. They fell away slowly into the mud. Black spots danced before my eyes and I kicked desperately, swimming toward what I hoped was the surface. In my last moments of consciousness, I felt powerful arms haul me out of the water and into clean air. Coughing, I clung to Marcus as he swam up and back to the shore and hauled us both out of the muddy water. He walked us toward the edge of the wood, a safe distance from the sinister lake that had just tried to eat me. I finished coughing up dirty water as he set me down on the ground.

"Thank you," I said, looking down; looking down at my feet. "They stole my boots!" I cried.

Marcus looked at me like I was crazy. "You nearly drowned, and you're upset about some boots?" he said.

I liked those boots—a lot. Saying so was only going to make me sound crazier at this point. Sighing, I looked at Marcus. "Let's go before something else tries to eat me," I said, limping away from the sprite-filled lake toward the market, quietly plotting revenge.

"Little shits! They bit my feet," I muttered.

Marcus came up behind me and scooped me up into his arms. "I'll carry you."

"Hey! Put me down! I can walk," I said in a voice that sounded whiny even to me. I couldn't help it. It had been a long day.

"No," he said.

"You could have at least asked," I pointed out, poking him hard in the chest.

"Fine," he said, putting me down. "May I carry you to the truck? So the walk back doesn't do more damage to your feet."

"No," I said stubbornly, taking a few small steps away. He crossed his arms and shook his head, slowly following behind me, matching my glacial pace. This was nuts. I was being ridiculous—this hurt.

"Fine, fine. I'm good to be carried now," I conceded. Dignity went out the window in favour of lessening the pain.

Marcus scooped me back up, cradling me to his chest, and strode swiftly in the direction we had come from. We passed through the market with no additional issues, quickly reaching the path to the road. As we walked, I relaxed into his strong arms. He smelled of mud and grass, which wasn't wholly unpleasant. Being carried around wasn't so bad, I guess. We arrived back at the truck in about a third of the time it took to get to the market.

As we approached the truck, I let Marcus have the keys in light of my lack of footwear. I slogged all the wet items into the bed of the truck with a thick thunk and shook off the worst of the dirt. I cringed as I took the passenger seat; my truck was so clean, it felt like sacrilege to bring this much muck into the cab. I leaned back, unhappy that this weekend was going to involve a lot of upholstery cleaning. Grabbing my phone, I sent my hacker friend a quick text asking if we could meet, before leaning back and closing my eyes. I had not used this much magic in a while; it had drained me more than I expected.

Marcus guided us back on the road, and we took off toward the house. As we approached, the turn to the lane that led up to the house, Marcus kept going straight toward the provincial park.

"Hey, you missed the turn," I said, annoyed. I wanted to shower, like, yesterday.

"Someone is following us," he said calmly, as if that was a totally normal thing to happen. I craned my neck around to peer out the back window. Behind us, there was a nondescript-looking white SUV with darkly tinted windows.

Turning back to the front, I asked, "So what do we do?" My

experience with being followed was precisely zero.

"I'll circle around the park entrance and head back to town. Hopefully, the additional witnesses will deter them enough so we can head back to the house without them." That sounded like an optimistic plan, given we were out in the middle of nowhere. I supposed that was better than no plan at all. Marcus pushed the speed, edging up to the top of the dial of my old truck. A quick glance behind told me they were catching up rapidly.

"Hold on," Marcus yelled over the noise of the engine. He jerked into the small parking area for a hiking trail and pulled the truck into a tight U-turn before speeding away. We passed the oncoming SUV with a whoosh. Before we could celebrate our escape, a blast of purple magic slammed into the side of the truck, quickly followed by a second and a third blast. The final one had ripped through a tire, leaving Marcus fighting for control of the truck.

The SUV careened alongside us, slamming into the passenger side door with a force that had my teeth rattling. The window shattered. A second slam sent us off the road, throwing me forward as stars exploded in my eyes.

The truck swerved, narrowly avoiding a tree, and landed heavily partway into the deep ditch. I groaned, pushing hair out of my face. My hand came away sticky with blood. Well, that can't be good, I thought. I leaned my head on the back of the seat to wait for the world to stop spinning. While I struggled to keep my eyes open, Marcus appeared outside my door. He violently tore it off the hinges and threw it into the mud of a bare cornfield.

I giggled. "You're strong." I clearly was not with it at the moment. My head rolled over to look at him as he undid my seat belt and pulled me from the truck.

"You need a hospital," he said. His statement jolted some sense back into me.

"No, I've got healing potions at home. No hospitals."

"You've been hit with a spell, and you're bleeding—we are going to a hospital," he said in a tone that brooked no argument.

"My house is closer, and healing potions will work better than a doctor," I said. Marcus growled something unintelligible at me while shrugging me closer to his chest.

He started down the road toward the house, hugging me closer. "Hold on, I'm going to run," he said, and he took off at a pace no human could have managed. Before I could adjust to the speed, we had arrived on the front porch. Marcus pushed open the front door and whisked me up the stairs to my apartment, placing me gently on the sofa. "Potions?" he asked.

"Under the bathroom sink, it's the silvery looking blue ones," I replied. He disappeared. While he was rummaging through the cabinet, Kit appeared and crawled up on my chest, whimpering quietly in worry.

"It's fine. I've had worse, remember," I told her soothingly, but it didn't seem to make a difference. Marcus reappeared, holding the box of potions I had made months ago. Silently thanking Past Me for her foresight, I sat up slowly and took the offered glass. I knocked it back like a shot and sat waiting for it to kick in.

Marcus took a seat on the coffee table in front of me and looked at my head expectantly. "It's not working," he said.

"Just give it a little while. It's magic, but not medical level magic," I said, as the ache in my head faded. "See, I'm feeling better already." I smiled weakly as I got up unsteadily, going to the bathroom to disinfect and bandage the cuts that were still oozing blood. "All I need is a shower and nap, and I'll be back to my normal level of irritating. Stop worrying," I called out to him.

Marcus harrumphed at me, looking unconvinced, as I wobbled back to the sitting room.

I plopped back down on my sofa and pulled out my phone. I wanted to text Abby about what had happened and tell her to be extra careful driving home tonight. I didn't get a response right away, but I willed myself not to worry. She was at work and probably not near her phone. Slightly cleaner and now bandaged up, I was starting to truly feel better. The healing potion and the injury had left me exhausted, but the pain had faded completely.

Marcus abandoned his perch on the coffee table, sitting down beside me, the small sofa not quite adequate to hold his enormous frame. He stretched out his legs.

I laughed. "You look ridiculous."

He scowled back at me. "Why is your sofa so small, anyway?" he grumped.

I laughed harder. "Because it's just me here. Why do I need a big sofa?"

His expression sobered. "You bought a small sofa with the intent of never sharing it with anyone?" He put his arms up on the back of the couch and shifted around, trying to get comfortable.

I had never thought about it like that before. He was right. I had never pictured myself here with anyone but Kit. I wondered what that said about me.

"I suppose I never really gave my furniture choices much thought."

He looked at me with a mock-serious expression. "Clearly. I'm here now—perhaps consider a larger sofa, or maybe even a beanbag chair over there in the corner for me?" At some point in the conversation, I felt like we had stopped talking about my furniture choices. I shifted on the couch, pulling my legs under me.

"Yes, but you are only here temporarily."

Marcus stopped shifting around and faced me. "Life is temporary, but that doesn't mean we shouldn't embrace the moment for fear of its passing," he said, sliding his hand up my bare arm, leaving goosebumps in its wake. His skin was rough against the smoothness of my arm.

I leaned into him, enjoying the comfort he offered me. Slowly, he inclined his lips toward mine. His kiss was warm and sweet, more of a promise of things to come. I melted into him, returning the kiss. He pulled away from me before gathering me into his arms.

I wondered what the hell was wrong with me, kissing him like that. I was crap at anything approaching romance; this would end in disaster for so many reasons. I finally acknowledged my exhaustion and settled into his broad chest, setting my worry aside for a time when I wasn't so tired. I soaked up the comfortable warmth of him as he wrapped his arms around me. I was briefly aware of him picking me up and carrying me to my bed sometime later before sleep fully claimed me.

Chapter 10

I woke groggily from the after-effects of the healing potion. Groaning softly, I rolled over and sat up. I caught a whiff of myself on the way and nearly gagged. My clothes were fermented with lake water and other things I would rather not think about. I dragged my sore body off the bed and headed straight to the bathroom. I piled my clothes in the corner. They were done. I would give them a Viking funeral later; fire was the only solution to that smell. I stood under the water, turning it to the hottest setting I could stand, and let it wash away the remaining dirt and blood. I felt like crap. Healing potions were great, but they did nothing for stress and the lingering soreness. I attacked my skin with soap and wore away several layers of skin, trying to excise the remaining evidence of my misadventure. Finally satisfied I was about as clean as I could get, I stepped out of the shower and wiped the mirror off to take an inventory of my injuries. I sighed. Well, at least I matched. I looked like shit, and I felt like shit. Great.

I shrugged on a comfortable wool sweater and jeans, trying not to wince at the various bruises. Running a brush through my hair and quickly pulling it into a loose braid, I felt clean. Finally ready to face the rest of the world, I headed down the stairs, following two voices I could hear coming from the living room.

I rounded the corner to find Marcus and Abby having a heated debate. "Milk bags again?" I interrupted. Kit hopped down from her spot on the mantle and rushed over to me. Picking her up, I sat down on the sofa beside Abby, pulling my legs up under me and placing Kit in my lap.

Abby glowered at me. "No, we're debating why someone has tried to kill you twice today!"

"Technically, it was only once. I feel like the sprites don't count, and it wasn't just me. Our friends in the SUV were after him, too," I said, waving my hand in Marcus's direction. "Also, it may not have been me at all. It could have been just Marcus they were after, seeing as it's his investigation. I'm just along for the ride."

Abby looked unconvinced.

Marcus interjected, "I don't think that's accurate. This investigation must be tied to you. The demon head was found on your lawn after all."

I sat back, considering that he was right. It had started before he had arrived. My phone buzzed from my pocket. My hacker friend had asked to meet tonight at Dragons Meet around nine. Glancing at the time, I saw that gave me an hour to get to the village. I had not slept all that long and was sure that would catch up with me soon.

"We can meet my friend in about an hour in the village," I said to Marcus. He nodded and headed upstairs without another word.

Abby turned to me, glaring. "So you seem to be having an adventure without me. More importantly, that sexy beast of a man seems to be very interested in you—and not in a professional way, which is very, very interesting. So spill.

Preferably right now." She looked at me expectantly.

"There isn't really anything else to tell. Marcus filled you in on the attacks, so you know what I know," I said, because while we had shared a moment earlier, there wasn't much else to tell. I wanted to sort out what I wanted to do about Marcus before sharing it with anyone else.

Abby humphed at me. "I doubt that, but it can wait. I feel like we have bigger problems right now." She got up and tossed her backpack over her shoulder. "I have to get to work now. Don't die, okay?"

I smiled at her ruefully. "Living was sort of my long-term plan," I replied.

She squeezed my shoulder on her way out of the room, the Abby-equivalent of a hug. I tried not to wince; I was still sore. I put Kit down on the floor and headed into the kitchen; I needed to eat something. Leaning on the counter, I listed off all the things I need to get done before we left to meet Logan. My truck, I assumed, was still in the ditch. It would need to be towed into the village and repaired. I did not know how I would come up with the money. I found my bag that Marcus had left on the counter and dug out my phone, scrolling through my contacts until I found the number for the mechanic, who assured me the truck would be back in the garage by the morning. As I hung up the phone, a wave of dizziness overtook me, and I slid to the floor. I was in worse shape than I had thought. Maybe I would just stay there on the floor until the walls stopped moving.

Marcus interrupted my inspection of the grout between the tiles crouching down in front of me. "Are you sure you're up for this?" he asked

I nodded, trying to summon the strength to get up off the

floor, when Marcus offered a hand. I took him up on the offer. I didn't think I was getting up without help at this point.

"Thanks," I said, finally making it to my feet. Marcus hesitated before reluctantly letting me go. I was grateful he didn't try to convince me to stay behind. I knew I was at my limit, but I was stubborn. I wanted answers, and I was convinced Logan could help us.

Logan and I had crossed paths years before when he had been deployed as our base tech analyst. He was brilliant with anything containing a computer chip; less brilliant with actual humans. We had bonded over our love of all things geeky and a shared disability when it came to understanding other people. He had left service when he found out his girlfriend had abandoned their daughter with his parents and disappeared. Logan was the one who had helped me buy Purple Hill three years before and supported me through Kit's first few months, which had been hard for both of us. I hated to drag him into this situation, but, as my best friend, I knew he would be more upset if I didn't ask him. That was just the sort of person he was.

"Let's go. Eating something will help." I said, grabbing my bag and heading for the door. "You can drive," I said, trying to be cheeky but sounding more tired than clever. The drive to the Meet was a quiet one. The sun had set, and every set of headlights made me wonder if we were going to be run off the road again.

We arrived without incident. Stepping into the heat of the pub made me feel incrementally better. I spotted Logan's tall, slim shape standing by the bar, talking to Brandon. The two of them were as thick as thieves, always coming up with outrageous plans that, more often than not, ended in some sort of trouble.

I approached them, slowly threading my way through the crowd. Marcus followed close behind, his hand out to steady me when I swayed. His closeness was disconcerting. Every time we touched, I was hyperaware of my tingling skin under his hands. I sat down heavily on a bar stool beside Logan, who had finally looked up from his conference with Brandon and noticed me.

"Alena, you look terrible," he said, concerned. Brandon nodded in agreement, placing a glass of water in front of me.

"I'm fine—just a long and exhausting day," I replied, though I don't think I was very convincing.

Marcus stood behind me, protectively greeting the others with a quick nod. Brandon, sensing the serious mood, left us to talk in privacy. We headed to the back of the bar to an out of the way booth. Sitting down, Marcus pulled out the phone and handed it to Logan, skipping the niceties.

"It's in pretty rough shape," Logan noted, flipping it over and pulling the cover off to inspect its insides. "What are you hoping to get off it?" he asked.

"Anything would be helpful," Marcus said.

While the two discussed technical elements of how to extract the data from the soggy phone, Brandon delivered a pot pie piled high with potatoes and vegetables.

While the other two were distracted by the technical elements, Brandon mouthed at me, "Everything okay?" pointing to Marcus and winking. I blushed and nodded. His grin widened at my discomfort before he mercifully let me eat in peace. I devoured the food like I had not eaten in days. The healing potion had really drained me. Feeling somewhat restored by the meal, I refocused my attention on the intense discussion between Marcus and Logan that I had been listening to with only half an ear.

"You need to understand the information I pull may not be useful. It seems to me like you're chasing something that may not exist. It could be a coincidence that the drugs were found here, not some overarching conspiracy as you suggest," Logan explained. I got the sense I had missed some crucial information while I had been stuffing my face.

"The truth is out there," Marcus said, totally deadpan.

Logan looked astounded. "Did you just quote *X-Files*?"

Marcus looked at Logan as if weighing his words carefully, then sighed. "See, this I will never understand," he said, looking annoyed. "People see me and think I'm a big, bad soulless—which I am—but somehow this means I can't have a Netflix account? It's obvious I live in a dark castle with no electricity or indoor plumbing, brooding about my dark fate." He took a deep breath before continuing on. "It's utterly impossible that I can rip a head off a demon with my bare hands, wield a flaming sword and still go home to my tastefully decorated flat in central London, have a shower with all the modern trappings and settle down to binge-watch something on Netflix?" He crossed his arms and sat back against the booth, looking disgruntled. "I like indoor plumbing, you know, and Netflix."

Logan took a moment, looking thoughtful. Seeming to have something in his brain finally click, he asked, "So... Star Trek or Star Wars?"

"Why choose?" Marcus asked, a hint of a smile returning to his face.

Logon carried on, unperturbed. "Marvel or DC?"

Marcus smiled slyly. "I'm sorry, those are some very intimate and revealing details of my life. We just met, after all—perhaps buy me a beer first?" he said.

"Okay. I can do that," said Logan, getting up to head to the bar for another round. "We are friends now," he stated, as if it was some indisputable fact, before walking away. To Logan, starting a friendship was an uncomplicated matter of black and white and did not require additional analysis.

Marcus looked perplexed. "Your friend is extraordinarily strange."

"Yes, he is. It's part of his charm." I paused, thinking for a moment; describing Logan to others was hard. He was exactly as he appeared, and that was sometimes strange for people. People rarely were as straightforward as him. It's part of the reason I enjoyed being his friend so much. There was never any subtext. "Logan is just as he appears, so yes, you have just gained a friend for life. Logan doesn't feel the need to complicate things with subtlety. He claims it's inefficient."

"I like it," he said as Logan returned with our drinks.

"What do you like?" Logan asked.

"Marvel," replied Marcus.

"Oh, good. It would have been a very short friendship otherwise," he said matter-of-factly as he sat down. Marcus barked out a laugh and took a long sip of his beer.

I laughed to myself, enjoying listening to the two of them banter back and forth. Having satisfied my hunger, my eyes were getting heavy. I dozed, leaning against Marcus to stay upright.

"I think Alena is nearly asleep. You should take her home before she passes out. I woke her up once, and she threw a book at me. It's not safe. Best get her back before it comes to that."

I glared at him, trying to form a denial, but my brain was fuzzy, and his assessment of the dangers of waking me being woken up was accurate. Hard to argue with the truth. Marcus got up, motioning for me to follow.

"Come on, let's get you home," he said, helping me to my feet.

Logan rose, too, giving me a quick hug. A rare thing from him, I must have looked worse than I thought if I was eliciting hugs from my friends. "I'll text you when I get something, though I may take a day or two," he said, taking one more look at me before pointing me toward the door where Marcus waited. I nodded and headed into the night. As I watched the stars overhead through the car window, my mind wandered to the evidence we had to go on, which wasn't much. I hoped Logan would have something new for us soon. I dozed curled up against the car door for a while before I was lifted out of my seat, still half-asleep.

Kit met us at the door, whining softly. Marcus paused, crouching down with me. "See, Kit, she's just tired. She will be okay, I promise. I'll take her up to bed now." Kit wove through his legs and dashed up the steps ahead of us, appeased I was going to be okay.

I snuggled into Marcus's hard chest as he carried me up the stairs. I let my hand slowly travel up to his neck and back down again, inhaling his spicy forest scent. Marcus let out a harsh breath, pulling me closer as we made it up to my apartment. "I seem to be getting carried around a lot today," I noted unhappily as he placed me on my bed.

"Nearly dying repeatedly will do that to a person," he said, removing my sneakers and tossing them on the floor.

The bed shifted under his weight as he sat beside me,

brushing some stray hair from my face. I leaned my head into his palm, and, grabbing his shirt, I pulled him closer. It seemed nearly dying had also made me bold. Reaching up, I pulled his lips to mine. My kiss was demanding. I wanted this right now and to hell with everything else. My hands slid up under his shirt, exploring the smooth skin beneath. Marcus pulled away, leaving a trail of soft kisses down my neck, while he teased my hardened nipples through my thin T-shirt.

"You need to sleep," he growled softly at me, clearly conflicted between desire and the necessity of sleeping.

"Mmmhmmm," I said, carrying on my exploration, ignoring him. I could always sleep later. This right here was much better. I nipped at his neck, and he gasped.

"Gods be damned, I should be sainted for this," he said, pulling away from me entirely and standing up. I huffed at the loss of heat, lips, and hands. He covered me with a blanket, and the last thing I felt was his soft lips on mine as sleep took me.

Chapter 11

A loud boom that I felt more than heard rattled through my body, throwing me to the ground. I coughed in the silver ash that covered the ground and fell softly like deadly snow from the sky. The unhuman screaming tore at my mind while I watched the magic consume living flesh from all it touched. Combatants, children, friends: it was uncaring of who its victims were. I lay paralyzed with terror as I watched it rolling in great heaving masses toward me. I saw my skin bubble and fall away with detached horror until the agony began. Finally, my frozen nerves came alive, registering what I was feeling; I screamed, the torment overwhelming my senses, leaving nothing but pain.

Panting, I jerked up from my nightmare, my eyes darting around frantically, hoping I had not woken Kit. Seeing she was still asleep in bed, I looked down at my hands to assure myself they were still there. The dreams were so real. Collapsing back down on my sweat-soaked pillow, I sighed. My body ached fiercely as I tried to still my racing mind, hoping that I would get some rest. I was still exhausted. I lay there watching the shadows cast by the moon dance across the ceiling.

Frustrated, I threw off the covers. I grabbed a cozy flannel robe that had seen better days and threw it around my shoulders. I would not sleep again any time tonight. My nightmares had gotten better since coming to Creemore, but they seemed to return with a vengeance when I was stressed. I crept softly over to where Kit was sleeping in her bed. She looked peaceful, but I pulled the baby monitor out of the bedside table just in case she had another night terror. I picked my way carefully through the dark apartment, heading down the stairs to the kitchen. My anxiety was running high with everything that was happening. Even the small noises of a tree branch tapping the window made me flinch. Tea would make me feel better. It always did.

I reached the main floor of the house, where the kitchen light was already on. Marcus was perched on a kitchen stool, working on his laptop. He had on a black T-shirt paired with thin sweatpants. His shirt left little to the imagination, but my imagination was having a field day, anyway.

"We need to stop meeting like this," I said, walking into the room and heading for the kettle.

Marcus looked up from his laptop, giving me a lingering look, taking in my long legs that currently weren't covered particularly well. His gaze made me instantly aware that I was in sleep shorts, tank top and an old robe, having woken earlier to change out of my jeans. Super sexy, that was me for sure.

"Feeling better?" he asked.

"Hmmm," I replied with a noncommittal noise, not wanting to admit I was still sore and tired.

"Can't sleep?" he asked.

"Not really," I said, leaning casually against the counter, trying to look like this midnight meeting wasn't making me preteen awkward. After my sleepy and unsuccessful attempt to lure Marcus into my bed had been rebuffed, I felt self-conscious of my boldness; it was out of character for me. I made a deliberate effort to bury my attraction to him and focus on my tea. The kettle clicked off, and I turned to grab a mug off the shelf. I heard Marcus get up behind me and turned quickly, clumsy, dropping the mug. In a blur, he caught it before it crashed into the ground. Standing up in front of me, he handed me the cup slowly. I nodded my thanks.

"Vampire speed is handy," I said. He was standing close enough for me to feel the warmth coming from his body.

Marcus looked at me with heat in his intense eyes. He reached up to touch my face softly, slowly lowering his lips to mine. His lips were warm and smooth. The moment they touched mine, the feelings I had been trying to ignore rushed to the surface. I kissed him back with urgency, my body demanding more. He responded by pushing closer to me until my back pressed against the counter. He parted my robe, sliding his firm hands inside it, tracing a path down from my waist to my hips with his fingers. I reached up to slide my arms around his neck as he lifted me up on the countertop. The cold stone on my thighs made me suck in a breath. He pulled back and leaned his forehead against mine.

"I want you."

There was a question in his voice. I wanted him. I wasn't sure if it was the right thing or the wrong thing, but I knew I would never regret taking the chance at this moment. I wanted to forget everything that had happened, all of it, just for a little while. I knew this wasn't any more than a fling, but right now, it was exactly what I needed. I ran my hands down his chest and back up under his shirt, gliding my hands across his hard-muscled back as he groaned softly into my neck.

"Good," I said, hoping that my inability to come up with a

more articulate remark wouldn't ruin the moment. Marcus lifted his head and kissed me ferociously. I returned it with equal amounts of enthusiasm. He pushed his hard length into the soft heat between my legs as I moaned his name.

"Hey, guys. Whoa," Abby said, coming to an abrupt halt in the entrance to the kitchen. Taking in the scene in front of her, she looked like a deer in the headlights.

"Fuck," he said into the crease of my neck, taking a deep breath, trying to collect himself. Marcus moved his hands away from their now abandoned exploration and put them at my sides on the counter.

"Abby, hey," I said, trying to sound calmer than I felt. My heart was racing. Well, this was not ideal. Marcus slowly took a small step away from me without letting go, looking unsure of what to say. He took the edges of my robe and tucked them together, at preserving the suggestion of modesty at least.

Abby's eyebrows had taken up residence high on her forehead. "You two are so busted," she snickered, heading to the fridge. "Guess I wasn't the only one who wanted a midnight snack." She wiggled her eyebrows suggestively at us.

I was going to kill her. Genuinely, she was one of my closest friends, but I was already pondering where to bury her body in the yard. I slid off the counter, pushing Marcus gently away to finish making the tea I had abandoned earlier.

"You're hilarious, Abby, truly hilarious," I said. She shrugged in response, grabbing some leftovers from dinner from the fridge.

"Well, you kids have fun," she said, as she beat a hasty retreat from the kitchen, still chuckling quietly to herself.

Marcus was still standing by the counter, an unreadable expression on his face. The spell had been broken. All that remained was an awkward silence. I looked down at my tea to see if the answers would be there. They were not. I sighed.

"I'm going to bed," I announced, turning to making a swift exit before he could say anything, my earlier confidence having long fled. Walking up the stairs to my apartment, I wondered if maybe I should ditch the tea for something more substantial, since clearly I wouldn't be sleeping again tonight. I had reached the landing outside the apartment door when I heard Marcus coming up the stairs behind me.

"Alena, please don't run from me," he said softly, catching up to me on the landing.

"I'm not running. I'm walking slowly." I heaved a sigh, turning to face him. "I'm not running from you. I'm running from myself." Yep, I didn't sound crazy at all. Nope, not me. Totally sane. I must have hit my head harder than I thought, because my brain clearly wasn't working anymore.

He smiled at me. "The physics of that may be challenging," he said, reaching for me.

I stepped toward him as if pulled by an invisible string. Marcus kissed me softly and the desire in my veins caught fire; I pulled him to me, pressing my aching core against his hardness, wrapping my arms around his neck. He backed us toward the window ledge. Working his hand under my shirt, he palmed my breast and roughly rubbed his thumb against my hard nipple.

"Maybe we should head inside?" he said, nodding to the door. He kissed me hard once more before lifting me up, and I wrapped my legs around his waist, desperate to keep contact with him. As we reached the door, a crash followed by a yelp of concern came from inside the apartment.

"You have got to be kidding me." Marcus sounded exasperated.

I laughed softly, hearing something falling to the floor with a loud crash. "Better go see what she's gotten into this time." I unwound myself from him.

Marcus looked at me ruefully. "This isn't over," he promised, kissing me like a man possessed once more, before turning and heading back down the stairs.

I wasn't sure if the tingling in my belly was a sign of excitement or dread. Marcus was getting under my skin in a way that I wasn't wholly comfortable with, but a part of me wanted him for more than just one night. I wasn't sure what to make of that. I saw the sun creeping over the horizon through the window, thinking that I might as well go see what Kit had gotten into and start the day. I had a feeling it was going to be another long one.

Chapter 12

After a long cold shower and having cleaned up the lamp Kit had broken, I headed downstairs, only to find the kitchen empty. Grabbing a coffee from the still-warm pot, I wandered into the also vacant living room. Where was everyone?

"Alena! We're out here," Abby yelled from the porch. Taking a sip of my coffee, I followed the direction of her voice. Pushing the front door open, I came up short.

"You have got to be fucking kidding me," I groaned. Facing me, rather gruesomely, was the upper body of a giant demon, strung up on the lawn like a scarecrow. Its eyes had been gouged out, leaving dark, unseeing hollows to stare at me. I shuddered. This was grossly out of my comfort zone. What the hell was going on?

Abby and Marcus were parked in the wicker chairs, casually sipping coffee, looking like they didn't have a care in the world.

"What do you think of our new lawn ornament? It's much more impressive than the first one, if you ask me," Abby said.

Marcus looked thoughtful for a moment before adding, "The eyes are a delicate touch. Very avant-garde."

"You two are insane," I said, unable to hold back my grimace at the smell wafting my way. While the situation was grim, it was hard not to find some amusement in the sheer bizarreness of it all. If it hadn't been for the attacks on us yesterday and the more significant issue of what was contained in the first body, this mystery might even have been entertaining, in a lousy horror movie kind of way. I realized maybe I needed some more positively engaging hobbies if this was what I now considered entertainment. Or a therapist. Probably both good options at this point.

"So, Mr Investigator, what do we do next?" I said, sitting down on the front steps.

"I'll test this one for the drugs. If it's negative, I suppose you could bury it in your garden. If I had to hazard a guess, I'd say it's full of the same compounds as the other one, given it's still here and not a pile of ash," he said, looking grim. "I think it's time for us to consider how to keep you safe until we get to the bottom of this." He got up from his chair, downing the last of the coffee. "I need to make some calls." Without further explanation, he strode into the house.

I sat there for a while longer, wracking my brain, trying to see a connection between the bodies and myself. There was nothing obvious—no enemies, no shady characters in my recent past, nothing to warrant the morbid scarecrows we were quickly acquiring. I wondered if this was related to my time in Special Projects, but promptly dismissed it. I had completely buried my identity, along with all of my personal ties, when I retired; no one would make that connection. I sighed, looking over at Abby.

"What do you think?" I asked her.

She looked concerned for a moment before getting up abruptly. "I don't know. I need to make some calls too," she said, heading for the door.

Now abandoned on the porch, the weight of the situation settled on me. If there was a danger here, I needed to make sure both Kit and Abby were safe before doing anything else. This seemed to be centred around the house, at the very least. So the next logical step would be to move Kit and Abby away for a while. Decision made, I texted Logan, asking him if he would let Kit stay with him until this was resolved. One down and one to go, I headed in to convince Abby to go there as well. It would be a hard sell; she was—like me—not one to run from danger.

I searched both the kitchen and the living room, but Abby was nowhere to be seen. Stepping out into the garden, I found Marcus pacing furiously along the stone pathway. He was having a very heated conversation with someone on the other end, and I wanted to give him some privacy. I turned to leave.

"Alena, wait," he called, waving me over. He disconnected the call abruptly, and the phone started ringing again before he could put it away. Looking at the screen, annoyed, he silenced the phone and shoved it in his pocket. "I need to go back to London," he said without preamble. "The powers that be feel that there isn't more to be found here," he huffed, clearly not agreeing with the assessment.

My disappointment at this announcement surprised me. I was hoping we would have more time together.

He ran a hand over his hair, looking frustrated. "You will come with me," he said. It didn't sound like a question.

"Why?" I asked, anger rising in me. I didn't like not being given a choice in the matter. "My life is here. I can't just drop everything and go to London." Really, if I thought about it, my life here didn't actually have many concrete commitments. I didn't mention this out loud, as part of me didn't want to admit that my life had become so disconnected from everything.

"This situation is linked to you somehow. I need to go back to London, so you will come with me," he barked, like I didn't already know this.

"That doesn't mean I need to leave. What's the sense in that?" I shot back. Even to my untrained ears, that logic sounded weak. I narrowed my eyes at him. "What's this really about?" I asked.

"I can't keep you safe if you're here!" he yelled at me.

My eyebrows shot up. I did not expect that. What was this going on? He was so even-tempered, even when faced with danger and uncertainty. I looked up at him. He seemed as surprised as me at his outburst.

"I'm sorry," he said, pulling me in close. "Just come with me, okay?" he asked softly, resting his chin on my head.

I leaned into his chest, trying to sort out my emotions. Part of me was pleased he wanted me to come, and I wasn't sure what to make of that. In my mind, Marcus was supposed to be a convenient fling, a distraction from the monotony. Not someone who felt the need to protect me. I looked up at him, studying his face and trying to find an answer in his eyes. Maybe I had misjudged the situation? I took a step back from him, needing some space. I sighed heavily.

"I'll come," I said, giving in. Because, if I was honest with myself, it made sense to leave. With Kit and Abby safe, my leaving might draw whoever was doing this away from Creemore. It would also give me an active role in finding out what the hell was going on. I was not willing to sit idly by while bodies piled up. Kit would be safe with Logan while I was gone, and I would make sure Abby was out of harm's way as well.

"I'll need to take Kit to Logan's place." I was saying it, so he understood that this wasn't a negotiation. He looked relieved I had agreed so quickly on this impromptu trip.

"Of course, though, if you want, I can pull some strings and try to get her some legitimate travel documents. There are a few perks to being with MCIB," he said. I thought about it for a moment before pushing it aside. I didn't know what I would walk into in London. It would make me feel better to have her with me, but it wasn't the safest option for her.

I shook my head. "No, Logan is better for her," I said, finally stepping back from the security of his arms, sad at the loss of warmth. "What about Abby?" I asked.

"What about Abby?" Abby said from her spot leaning against the door frame, making a face at Marcus and me.

"Marcus has to go back to London. I'm going to go with him," I explained. I wanted Abby to come with us. Leaving her here alone didn't sit well with me. Abby looked relieved at my declaration, which was strange. Why would she be glad we were leaving? I pushed it aside. I was probably just being overly suspicious; this situation had me on edge.

"Well, I'm certainly not going to London, if that's what you're thinking," she said, as if reading my mind. "I'll stay here and guard the house, obviously. Someone has to water the plants." And with that, she spun on her heel, marching back into the house. Okay, that was odd—even for Abby.

Marcus's phone started buzzing again in his pocket. He reached for it, shooting me an apologetic look as he answered it. I nodded and went after Abby. Her weirdness required some explanation. I found her sprawled out on the couch, reading a novel. I sat down opposite her, leaning my elbows on my knees and stared at her intently until she finally sighed and put her book down.

"You're being weird," I said.

"I am weird," she said, lifting her book again. I went back to staring at her. "What?" she said, annoyed.

"Weirder than normal."

Abby sighed, sitting up. "Look, it's fine. I'll be safe here. I know we don't share much about our time before coming here, but be sure I've got enough skills to keep myself safe." She paused. "I've got enough power in my pinky finger to blow up the house if I really want." She lay back down again. "If anyone comes here and tries to mess with me, I'll just do this and blow them to smithereens," she said, wiggling her little finger at me over her book.

I snorted. I had the feeling this wasn't an argument I was going to win. Sighing resignedly, I got up. I needed to get Kit packed up and throw some things together for myself. I didn't like this, but I had to trust her judgement.

"Fine, but don't blow up the house, okay?" I shot over my shoulder.

"No promises, so come back soon," she shouted after me. "Hey, Alena." I turned, surprised that her tone had gone serious. "Maybe live a little? Marcus seems like good people. He may not be forever material, but that doesn't mean you can't have some fun. Stop hiding in this big old house all alone."

I turned and left without replying. Her sentiment echoed Marcus's comments earlier: was I really just existing and not living? I was starting to think they were right. I needed more than just this house. I promised myself that when this debacle was over, I would make some changes.

Chapter 13

Kit had taken the news of her temporary relocation well. She was bouncing by the front door, eager to leave for Logan's, and acting like it was a grand adventure. I was a little hurt that she wasn't at least slightly upset at my departing, though I was not surprised: Logan's daughter Sofie was around the same age as Kit and treated her like she was a perfectly normal shifter child. The inability to shift or speak didn't seem to slow them down at all. The two of them got into all sorts of mischief when together.

Kit's blanket and some snacks sat by the door while we waited for Logan to arrive. We moved outside to sit on the porch together. I looked out at the yard and realized that while I had been upstairs getting everyone packed; it had been cleaned up. I was eternally grateful I wasn't the one who had to do it. One gross dead demon was enough for me. Abby told me that Marcus had tested the body while waiting for me to get Kit ready to go. It had behaved in the same way as the other one. The minuscule hope of it being something else was gone. Whatever I was mixed up in didn't seem to be going away.

I hadn't seen Marcus since we had spoken in the garden. I wondered what he had planned for our travel. It was getting close to lunchtime, but he seemed to think we would make it to London by evening, which meant we would travel by gate—something I was not looking forward to. I was getting queasy just thinking about it.

At the sounds of gravel crunching, I looked up, watching Logan's green truck pull up the driveway. Sofie jumped out and ran shrieking toward me. I met her halfway and swung her around, happy to get caught up in her silly excitement for a moment. Kit bounced around my ankles, making happy yipping sounds. I put Sofie down, and the two of them took off squealing around the side of the house toward the garden. I smiled at the sight of the two of them together. It warmed my heart to see Kit acting like the child she was. Even if she was a fox on the outside, she was still human on the inside. Logan approached the porch and sat on the steps. I walked over to join him.

"So, London, eh?" he asked.

"Yep."

"Kit will be safe with us," he said thoughtfully.

I knew without a doubt that Logan would keep her safe. He was human, but it never really mattered in the grand scheme of things; what he lacked in magic he made up for in intelligence and resourcefulness. He would treat Kit as his own, and for that, I was grateful beyond words.

"I know."

We sat there quietly, listening to the sounds of giggling coming from the back garden. The peace of the moment was broken by Marcus pushing through the front door, carrying his bags toward the SUV.

"You ready to go?" he asked, nodding hello at Logan.

"As ready as I'll ever be." I wasn't excited about this trip, but it was too late for second-guessing now. "Let me say goodbye to Kit, and I'll meet you in the car."

Logan and I got up and headed toward the riotous noises being made behind the house. Rounding the corner, we found Kit covered in mud and Sofie handling the hose, trying to get her clean. I couldn't stop the laugh that bubbled up. These two could cause trouble anywhere. Mud or no, I waved Kit over, giving her a squeeze.

"Be good for Logan," I said, "I'll see you soon, okay?" she nodded, looking over her shoulder, keen to get back to the game with Sofie. I gave her another quick hug and waved goodbye to them all, heading to the SUV where Marcus was waiting.

As we drove away, I stared at the ceiling of the car, fighting back the water pooling in my eyes. I had never left Kit before. I was worrying about things that weren't even rational, driving myself half-crazy, when a soft hand covered mine. Marcus gave me a comforting squeeze, saying nothing. It was a small comfort. Still, it calmed my mind enough that I didn't feel overwhelmed anymore. I gave him a small smile of thanks.

"So, do you have a plan, or are we making this up as we go?" I asked, pulling away from him, wanting to focus my mind on something else.

"My boss wants a briefing on what happened here as soon as possible. Depending on when we arrive in London, we'll go there first. The rest I plan to make up as I go," he said with a mischievous grin. "More fun that way."

I sat back, trying to do the math in my head. It was lunchtime here; when we arrived in London, it would probably be late evening. Gate travel wasn't always instantaneous or reliable. I wondered what to expect from a meeting with the higher-ups of the Magic Council's investigative branch. My only experience with the council so far was with Alrick, who, while a stickler for rules, was never one to stand on formalities. Lost in my own thoughts, the rest of the drive to Toronto went by quickly.

We pulled into a raised parking garage just as the sky opened up, pouring rain down by the bucketful. Stretching my legs from the long drive, I grabbed my bag and lamented my lack of an umbrella. I was going to get soaked. We dashed through the rain-soaked laneways toward the monolithic Union Station. The recent renovations had brought life back to the old structure; the glass and stone building stood bright against the stormy sky.

We moved through the crowded station down to the lower departure level, where the gate system connected with others all over the world. Centuries old, the system was a type of magically stabilized wormhole between several locations. You would purchase a unique token for your trip, step through the gate, and arrive, most of the time, instantaneously at your destination. It was prohibitively expensive. Only the desperate or wealthy used the gates and only for long distances, where it was not practical to use other forms of transportation. This is why most gates were housed in large cities and train stations; to enable connections between one system and the other.

I had only travelled via gate a few times, but my memories were not good ones. They had a tendency to make me violently ill. I hoped this time would be the exception to the rule. I didn't think throwing up on Marcus would come off as particularly entertaining.

I glanced toward the end of the hall. The gates were about twenty-five feet wide, their shimmering surfaces contained in thin metal frames. These were beautifully woven, with intricate spells carved into the metalwork to keep the gate stable. It would be beautiful if it wasn't so terrifying. Marcus handed me a token that would send me to London, and we joined the line of people waiting to go through. I fidgeted nervously, trying to appear calm and collected. Don't barf, don't barf, I chanted inside my head.

Marcus finally noticed my strange behaviour and looked concerned. "You've travelled by gate before, haven't you?"

"Yes." I swallowed heavily. "It's just I tend to get sick," I admitted, looking anywhere but his face.

"Oh. Well, that's okay. If you vomit, aim for my shoes. They were pretty much ruined in the lake, anyway." He looked down ruefully at the water-stained leather.

"At least you still have shoes," I said, still grumpy about the loss of my boots. The line in front of us had disappeared, and it was our turn to step through.

"Okay, I'll go first and meet you on the other side. Remember, hit my shoes, not my coat—I like this coat a lot." With a quick squeeze of my hand, he stepped through and was gone.

Clutching my token in a white-knuckled grasp, I closed my eyes and took a step through the shimmering surface.

Chapter 14

The sounds of London Bridge station assaulted me as I came through the disorienting experience of travelling through a magical wormhole. I walked unsteadily away from the gate, bile rising in my throat. Swallowing rapidly, hoping to keep the contents of my stomach where they belonged, I became surer of my footing the further away from the gate I got, and the worst of my nausea faded.

Finally looking up, I saw Marcus waiting for me and headed to meet him.

"Remember—my shoes, not the coat," he said, taking in my still slightly green face.

I snorted and flipped him off, annoyed that he seemed perfectly fine.

Together, we headed toward the sidewalk, where he flagged down a taxi. Our arrival had been later in the evening than I expected, but the streets of London seethed with a mass of humanity. I had never liked London. The noise, the smells and the ever on-the-go population had always grated on my nerves. The car behind us backfired loudly like a gunshot, and I flinched. I sat in the taxi clutching my bag tightly as if to protect myself from the city.

Marcus looked over at me. "I thought you might want to rest at my flat tonight before facing the inquisition at MCIB tomorrow."

My eyebrows crept up. I wondered if there was more to this offer than just rest.

Noticing my expression, he looked at me, feigning innocence and holding up his hands in protest. "I meant to actually clean up and sleep before heading into the office. It's pretty late." He paused for effect. "Unless you want to Netflix and chill?" he said, winking at me ridiculously.

I couldn't help but laugh, and some of my anxiety slipped away.

Marcus smiled back at me, taking my hand. "I'll take that as a yes, then?" he asked.

I thought about it: would spending the night with him be something I would regret? Looking him over critically, I thought probably not. Abby was right, and I should just take the chance with him. It wouldn't be the thing that solved my problems, but it would absolutely stir things up a bit.

"I'm not sure I know how to Netflix and chill," I said, smiling my best innocent face back at him. "I'm intrigued—it sounds relaxing." I said, hoping he would read between the lines. I really sucked at flirting.

Marcus's gaze turned heated, clearly understanding my awkward attempt at subtext. He rubbed the top of my hand, pulling me closer. I pressed myself into him, sliding my hands under his coat, warming my icy hands. Marcus hissed in a breath at the cold touch and my boldness. He looked at me like he was going to devour me in the back of the taxi. Leaning over, he kissed me—softly at first, but then more urgently. The heat of his kiss made me shudder with desire. Having finally chosen to give in to the attraction I felt and take the chance, seemed to have opened the floodgates, and I was happily drowning.

"Oi, mate, we're here," the taxi driver announced with an awkward cough, shattering the haze of kisses we were lost in.

Marcus pulled away reluctantly. "We are cursed to be constantly interrupted. I'm not sure who hates me so much to cast such a curse, but I will find them and end them swiftly," he said.

"I'll gladly help," I chuckled, though I was secretly glad of the interruption for a moment there. I had forgotten where we were and was thinking the taxi driver wouldn't have appreciated the show we had almost put on.

Standing on the rainy sidewalk, I looked up at the building. Marcus's apartment wasn't what I had expected, being in a quieter northern neighbourhood that was clearly going through a revival. The building had been a factory in a previous life but had been restored meticulously with accents of raw copper and black steel. We took the elevator up to the top floor that exited inside the flat. I was greeted by warm tones and comfortable looking furniture that was scattered around the large open-plan living room. I set my bag down and headed toward the wall of windows overlooking the sparkling night lights of London.

"Curry?" he asked, already dialling for takeout.

My stomach growled in response; suddenly, I was starving. Marcus joined me by the windows, pulling me toward him. I leaned my back against his tall frame as he encircled me with his arms.

"Is this your first time in London?" he asked without letting me go. It was an innocent question. He had no way of knowing that London was Pandora's box of memories for me.

I repressed my shudder at the memories that I had locked away in a dark corner of my brain, but they screamed at me to come out and play. With my attention redirected to darker topics, the earlier spell of warmth and desire faded away. I stepped away from him, putting some physical distance between us. Gazing out the window at nothing in particular, I breathed deeply and calmed myself.

"I was here briefly as a child," I answered vaguely.

Marcus gave my hand a light squeeze, as if sensing this was a topic I did not want to explore.

I turned to face him. "Did you grow up here?"

"No, I grew up in Germany. I came to London for school and just never left." He didn't elaborate on the rather vague explanation.

There was buzz announcing that the food had arrived. While Marcus was setting everything up on the coffee table, I wandered around the flat. Everything was impersonal, with no photos or knick-knacks. He either spent little time here or didn't want to display his personal life to visitors. I peeked into the bathroom, remembering his earlier conversation with Logan and noting he did, in fact, have indoor plumbing. I wondered what type of visitors he had here.

"Come eat," Marcus called, cutting short my snooping.

He handed me a plate, and I filled it with some of everything. I was starved. Lack of sleep and regular meals were not something my body approved of. When I had satisfied the worst of my hunger, I found Marcus studying me carefully, already having finished his meal. He looked more at ease there than anywhere else I had seen him, stretched out, arm draped over the back of the large sofa we were sharing.

"So, what do you think?" he asked.

"Well, you have indoor plumbing, so I suppose that's one more stereotype debunked," I replied, getting comfortable on the dark sofa.

"I mean the investigation. I don't spend too much time here, so I haven't had much of a reason to make anything of it. Though indoor plumbing is a step up from my standard castle and chamber pot."

I rolled my eyes at him, though I felt bad for judging him on his decor choices rather than who he was.

"It's fine," he said. "I'm used to it. Being Soulless has all sorts of baggage. Most people think we're barely sane killers. Then there's a small minority that thinks that we're romantically dark creatures in need of a mate."

He got up, restless, moving toward the kitchen. I heard the fridge open and close as he reappeared, carrying two beers. He handed me one and took the seat across from me, as if some distance would make it easier to talk about the problems he lived with.

"It's hard to dispel the myths, too, since they're based on a version of the truth," he said, taking a long sip of the beer. "The one about mates is fairly accurate," he said unhappily. "If my soulbound mate appears tomorrow, I belong to them regardless of anything else. What's worse, I'll supposedly be happy about it. If I lose the rings that bind me, I'll be trapped forever. I won't even be me anymore. I can't imagine how it's possible to have such fundamental choices taken away from you and be happy about it," he snorted angrily. "Luckily, it's unlikely—there are so few of us, and I avoid the annual match balls like the plague. Despite my family's meddling."

At the mention of his family, his expression lightened. I wanted to ask about them, but my attention focused first on something else he had said.

"Wait? What, the soulless have a singles night? Really?" I said. The idea of him in a tuxedo made my belly flip. It would be a sight I wouldn't mind seeing, but a soulless singles mixer seemed so strange to me, even if it made a sort of sense.

"I suppose it is essentially a singles night, though don't let anyone hear you say that—it's taken far too seriously by those who attend."

He looked sad for a moment, before the expression was hidden away behind the casual smile he always wore. I wondered what the story was there. It must be hard to be an outsider from your own people. Being neither part of vampire society nor the ranks of angels would be challenging, but to also reject a place among the soulless seemed a lonely place to be.

He turned to me, and I saw his gaze was conflicted. "I can't promise you anything beyond right now. I can't even promise I won't hurt you. I don't know where this thing with us will go, but I need you to understand that there are limitations to what I can give you." He got up, crossing the small space to sit beside me. I sat up, reaching for him, and our lips connected. His kiss was not urgent, but lingering. Tasting slowly, he leaned on me and then pulled away. "I don't want to hurt you, but there is a real possibility I will. I am not a good enough man to stay away, though." He held me in his arms, and I leaned my head on his chest, listening to his steady heartbeat.

There was so much to sort through, I didn't even know where to start. I yawned without thinking. Marcus stood up, pulling me with him.

"You're tired," he said, stating the obvious. "I'll set you up in the guest room," he said, and he walked away. I had a feeling I wasn't the only one who had a lot on their mind. Some distance had appeared between us, and I didn't like it. I followed him down the short hallway to the bedroom. He gave me a quick kiss goodnight and was gone like a ghost.

I closed the door and leaned into its supportive frame. Heaving a breath, I felt water pool in my eyes. I pushed the feelings away; I didn't want to process them tonight. Being back in London, being away from Kit, the complicated 'thing' I was falling into with Marcus—it was just too much for my tired brain to process. I took off my clothes and crawled between the soft sheets. It was a long time before I managed to fall asleep.

Chapter 15

I sat beside a stoic Marcus in the back of a black cab, drinking rich coffee and watching the busy streets of London zip by. We had woken early, getting ready and heading out before the sun had fully cleared the horizon. I had a feeling both of us wanted to escape the intimate environment of his apartment. Our conversation last night had given me pause, risking a quick glance at Marcus as he scrolled through his phone. His expression was one emotionless focus. I took another sip of the coffee, leaning back. I got the sense he was assuming my silence meant that I had reconsidered pursuing something with him.

I hadn't. As I lay awake the night before, I'd had time to think; despite the risks of future heartache, I still wanted him. Knowing everything now, and despite the risks of future heartache, I still wanted him. It was illogical and foolish, but somehow it didn't matter to me anymore. He made me feel good with him I laughed more, felt more, and I sensed this was the first step out toward a life that was living and not just existing. I had survived so much already. To sit back and play it safe, never taking chances, made me mad at myself for wasting a second chance that had come at such a high cost. It was a dishonour to those who had sacrificed everything so I could live.

I felt Marcus's eyes on me and turned to him. I wanted to show him I would not walk away from this, but had no idea how to do it.

"Marcus..." I started softly, trying to sound conciliatory, but he interrupted me.

"It's fine, I understand." He looked back at his phone, disappointment flashing across his features before being smothered by that blank, neutral expression I was starting to hate. Annoyance at the interruption rose up, and I embraced it. I was good at being annoyed and angry; this, I could use.

"Look, you foolish man, don't interrupt me," I said sharply.

That got his attention. He looked up, surprised at my tone.

"I'm not going to run screaming from you, okay? So stop with the stoic bullshit. It's annoying," I humphed, taking an angry sip of my coffee. "I can't make any promises either—I've nothing to offer you, and I'm not good at... people, let alone any sort of romantic relationship." I carried on before I lost my nerve. "You're not *that* special, with all your soulless baggage. I have baggage too." I shrugged. "If you can accept mine, I'm fine with yours. Though we may need a cart for all the extras." I was pleased I'd got that all out, and it made some sort of sense. I looked at Marcus, waiting for him to say something.

Marcus took one look at my earnest face and burst into laughter. It wasn't what I was going for, but it was better than nothing. I smiled back at him. He pulled me across the seat, careful not to spill my coffee.

"You always surprise me." Without further discussion, he kissed me deeply. He ran his hand through my hair, sending tingles down my spine. He pulled away as the taxi came to a halt. "I'm glad you're not going to run off, but I feel like we should revisit the screaming part. That might be something I could help you with." His roguish grin lit up his face, his eyes burning with promise. He pulled me back to him for another demanding kiss before letting me go.

I stepped out of the taxi and looked up. The Shard, with its monolithic glass walls and imposing structure, loomed over me. Of course, the Magic Council's investigative branch would be housed in the most prestigious building of London's skyline. I was impressed, craning my neck around like an eager tourist as Marcus led me to the stairs leading to the office entrance. We entered the lobby with its floor-to-ceiling white marble and slick modern design. We entered the lobby, with its floor to ceiling white marble and slick modern design, and headed for the elevator. Moments later, we were stepping into an open-plan office that was a hive of activity; creatures of all types bustled around the space purposefully, surrounded by high-tech office equipment.

I had half expected a castle with old men in robes chanting spells in a cloud of incense. This modern tech-heavy office was a pleasant surprise. I followed Marcus through the reception area to a block of conference rooms and offices. We stopped in front of one where it looked like a meeting was already in progress.

Marcus turned to me, asking softly, "Ready?" I nodded, and he pushed on the glass door. Every head in the room swivelled toward us as the room went silent.

An annoyed-looking woman stood in front of a giant screen on which technical data was scrolling by. She was of average height, her slim build spoke of strength, long jet black hair pulled back in a severe bun made her look older than I imagine she was. Her gaze was intense and cold, holding no welcome for us.

"Marcus, so kind of you to finally join us. Sit." She pointed to two seats at the front of the wide table, which were quickly vacated by the occupants.

I threaded my way through the cramped space and took my seat, not enjoying the eyes on me. I stared at my hands as the woman continued her briefing. After the first few minutes, I zoned out. Whatever we were being briefed on went completely over my head.. When she finally dismissed the others, she pointed a perfectly manicured finger at us.

"You two stay put."

We waited for everyone else to leave before she turned her full attention on us.

"I am Eleonore Ainsworth, head of intelligence. Who are you?" she asked, her gaze assessing me critically.

"This is Alena—" Marcus said before I could open my mouth.

"Zip it, Marcus. I'm positive she can speak for herself," Eleonore cut him off abruptly. I smiled to myself. This woman was terrifying, but I liked her already.

"Alena MacKenzie, former military intelligence and Special Projects Division. Currently, the Magic Council representative for Clearview Township," I said, falling back on my formal military training, hoping that it would lend some credibility to my presence here.

She narrowed her eyes at me. "Special Projects? That wasn't covered in your file." She glanced down at a folder on the desk.

So she had known who I was before I walked in here. I was annoyed with her games. Special Projects were off the official books, but it was an open secret. I wondered briefly why the information was being held back from the head of intelligence for the council. The human military holding back information from MCIB was unusual. I pushed the thoughts away. I was no longer responsible for the goings-on of Special Projects. I focused back on the woman in front of me.

"MacKenzie? Any relation to Celeste MacKenzie?" she asked, though it didn't sound like a question. It would seem she had connected the dots about my family name and history faster than most people.

"Yes, ma'am, she's my mother," I replied.

"Interesting. Marcus has a reluctance to work with anyone I assign to him. Given he seems to tolerate you, I will overlook your presence here for now. Understand, though: if you fuck up, I will ship you back to whatever backwater you came from." She didn't wait for my response before carrying on. "Now tell me everything."

Marcus gave her a briefing on everything that happened thus far, which wasn't much. When he was finished, Eleonore looked disappointed.

"That's not anything we didn't already know. Damn." She finally sat down at the head of the table. "I was hoping for more. I am not happy you gave the phone away. It's on your head if this person doesn't come through."

"What about the Oracle?" Marcus suggested, changing the subject away from Logan. "We've used that avenue before with some excellent results. It's not perfect, but it may give us some direction." The Oracle was a magical being that could travel between the planes of reality and see some of what has been or what is to come. I could see why it would be helpful when an investigation had run aground, but I was not excited about the idea. The Oracle and I had a complicated history.

"That is an excellent suggestion," Eleonore said. She got up and started pacing. "However, the Oracle is on sabbatical indefinitely." She shot me a pointed look.

I got her unspoken message loud and clear. This was going to suck, but she was right. It *was* a good idea. I sighed, resigned to my fate. I looked down at my phone, firing off a quick text as they discussed other options. A response pinged back right away, and I smiled. Perhaps this wouldn't be so bad after all.

"We can see the Oracle tomorrow morning if you like, though we'll have to go to Crosskirk in Scotland for the meeting," I said, interrupting their intense brainstorming session. Both of them looked at me.

"Good," Eleonore said, unsurprised and looking smug.

Marcus also looked surprised at my announcement, but quickly recovered. "We can leave now. We should be able to reach the Highlands by morning," he said, checking the time on his phone.

"Fine," agreed Eleonore, still looking at me suspiciously. "I expect a full report on what you discover." She swept out of the room without another word. I let out the breath I didn't know I had been holding and relaxed into my chair.

Marcus grinned at me. "You impressed her. Though I have questions about how you seem to know the Oracle. Always full of surprises, aren't you?" he chuckled to himself, standing and heading toward the door. I followed behind him, glad to be leaving.

"Let's get going, then. We need a few things from the flat, then we can head to the gate and arrive in Edinburgh by teatime." Marcus said, I tried to look optimistic about the prospect of travelling so soon. Still, another trip through the gate already had my stomach churning. It wasn't just the trip that had me nervous. The Oracle could help this investigation, but it also meant putting my secrets on display for Marcus to see. I was hoping my instinct to trust him was a good one, or I would have more significant problems to worry about.

Chapter 16

I stumbled out of the gate into Edinburgh's Waverley station, still not used to the falling sensation caused by gate travel. A warm hand steadied my shoulder before I could fall on my ass. Marcus stood behind me, looking concerned.

"I'm fine," I assured him, glad that the wave of nausea had subsided quickly this time. "Just not used to gate travel still." This seemed to appease him for the moment. He'd been overly attentive since we had left the Shard, and it was starting to feel oppressive. "Marcus, what's going on?"

He looked at me, confused. "What do you mean?"

"You're acting like I'm about to break apart at the next strong breeze," I said. I was trying to be calm, fighting down the chafing anger. I did not like people being protective of me. I did not like causing other people's protective instincts. I felt that made me responsible for the outcome somehow, outcomes that had traditionally ended badly. I knew it was twisted logic, but it was my truth –regardless of the dysfunctionality of it.

Marcus didn't answer me as we started toward the car rental kiosk. I sighed internally. I wasn't going to get an answer to this, was I? Fine. Whatever. I would not pout about it. Whatever was going on with us could wait. I should focus on the whole *save the world* mission we were on. Sitting on the bench outside the kiosk, I fiddled with my phone while I waited for Marcus to get our car sorted out. The situation in America between humans and the magical community had gotten progressively worse in the past few weeks. I was engrossed in an article about a recent anti-magic protest in DC that had gotten violent when Marcus sat down beside me.

"I don't know what's going on," he said, staring straight ahead.

"What?" I glanced up from my phone, not sure what he was talking about, my brain still distracted by the turmoil in America.

"I don't know what's going on," he repeated, finally turning to look at me. "I don't know why I'm overly protective of you. I'm sorry if it's bothering you. If it helps, it's confusing me too. I know you can handle yourself."

I didn't really know what to make of his admission. It was comforting to know that I wasn't the only one who didn't seem to understand how to navigate the new dynamic between us. I liked Marcus a lot, but relationships were never something I was very good at. Add to that the complicated situation of me being a witch and him a soulless, and it should be clear why I thought it was best to cut us both some slack while we figured this out. If I was honest with myself, despite the deck stacked against us, I wanted to make this work somehow, even if it was only for a short time.

"Okay," I said, standing up. "I can live with that for now." I smiled at him. "Come on, let's go. It's a long drive to Crosskirk."

"Are you going to tell me why the Oracle agreed to meet us in the Highlands and how you managed to get us this mysterious meeting with someone who is virtually inaccessible?" he said, heading toward our rental car.

"Nope, it's more fun this way." I grinned at him as I slid into the passenger seat. My grin got wider as I looked over at him; his annoyance was plain to see.

It was early afternoon, and the traffic wasn't too bad getting out of Edinburgh. Before long, we were speeding up the highway toward Inverness. The noise of the engine soothed me into a restless sleep.

***

"Hey," Marcus whispered, gently shaking my shoulder. "We're in Inverness. We're stopping here for the night. I know how much you need a proper bed." He said with a sly smirk.

"Good idea," I replied groggily. I was more tired than I thought, wondering when was the last time I'd had a full night's sleep. I looked out the window. Sometime after leaving Edinburgh, a fine drizzle had started and had given the tree-lined street a gloomy feel. In the distance, I could see Inverness Castle across the River Ness. Opening the door, I pulled my coat tighter around me. The temperature had dropped. Spring in Scotland was still basically winter, as far as I was concerned. Marcus went to the trunk and grabbed our bags before dashing across the street toward a gothic-looking stone townhouse. I pulled my hood up against the strengthening rain and jogged after Marcus, who was waiting for me in the house entranceway.

He took my coat, hanging it on a hook in the small vestibule. I shivered from the sudden chill, and he pulled me in, rubbing my arms to warm them.

"You're frozen," he said, like I hadn't noticed. His touch gave me goosebumps. "Let's get you warm," he said, his eyes glittering as he lowered his mouth to mine.

I reached up for him. This was a much better idea than the sweater I had planned. What had started as a quick kiss now escalated rapidly. While we couldn't quite figure out what we were doing, we didn't seem to lack passion; I suppose that was something. He reached behind me to grab my ass, lifting one leg and wrapping it around his waist. Pushed against the wall, I ground into him, having shed the cold in favour of heat that made me want to shed my clothing. I groaned as he pushed his erection against me. He nuzzled my neck.

"Bed? Upstairs?" he asked.

"Yes, now," I said breathlessly. We moved toward the wide staircase leading up to the second floor.

"If you two youngins are about finished there, would you like to join me for a drink?" a voice asked from the direction of a crackling fire I hadn't noticed.

Marcus let go of me, giving a rueful grin. "This is becoming a very unpleasant theme for us," he said.

I smiled back at him, amused; it seemed we couldn't get our timing right no matter what we did. The interruptus curse had struck again. I looked past his shoulder to locate the source of our current obtrusion. Sitting beside the massive fireplace was a grizzled old man, fiery red hair and beard glinted in the firelight. He reminded me of the Highlanders found on the cover of romance novels: strong, noble, and fierce. Marcus and I made some quick adjustments to our dishevelled clothing and stepped into the room.

The fire gave out a welcome warmth in the dreary, chilly night. Our host motioned to the chairs beside him, and he got up, heading toward the cellarette.

"Master Friedrich, I am very keen to hear what has brought

you to Inverness," he said pointedly. "And who your charming companion is," he added in a softer tone while bringing us both a finger of glistening amber liquid. I took a seat in the old wingback chair closest to the fire as he handed me my glass.

"Alabaster," Marcus said, bowing shallowly before being engulfed in a bear hug from the much larger man.

"Good grief, Marcus. It's good to see you again," he said, his smile lighting up his face.

Marcus grinned back, taking the proffered drink and throwing it back quickly. He handed the empty glass to Alabaster with a conspiratorial grin.

"Now introductions, Marcus—or do you still lack basic manners?" Alabaster turned his gaze on me.

"This is Alena MacKenzie. Alena, this is Alabaster Greely, head of the vampire clan here in Scotland," Marcus said, taking a seat opposite the chair Alabaster had returned to.

Alabaster looked at me with a more discerning look. "You're Celeste's girl, then?"

I nodded, wondering how he knew my mother; it seemed there was a lot of that happening today. "You know my mum?" Alabaster put his feet up on the ottoman and regarded his drink thoughtfully. "Ay, I do. We got into all sorts of trouble in our younger days. She was a right pain in the arse. Bossing people around, doing whatever she felt like without so much as a 'by your leave' to the rest of us." He chuckled to himself. "Full of fire, that one. She's helped me out a time or two, though. We've not seen much of her since she met that William of hers and disappeared." He looked at me questioningly. "You wouldn't mind telling a lonely old man where she's gone off to, would you?"

I studied him for a moment, wondering what to say. My

mother was a recluse by choice, and I understood her reasoning well. If she didn't trust this man to tell him where she was, I wasn't going to enlighten him.

"If you know my mum well, you'll know telling her secrets will get you a tongue lashing you'll not soon forget—or worse. I'm afraid you'll just need to embrace a little mystery in your life." I took a sip of my drink, trying not to look uncomfortable with the conversation.

Alabaster let out a roar of laughter, slapping his leg repeatedly.

"Oh ay, I do, I do—she's told me off more times than I can remember! She can have her secrets—you're a good lass for keeping them," he said when he finally stopped chuckling. His expression turned serious for a moment. "Though when you see your ma next, remind her that Molly and I would like to see her, if she would be so kind as to grace us with her presence." He paused, thinking. "I've a keepsake of hers that I think she may wish returned."

Marcus watched the exchange with curiosity, sipping his second drink, no doubt wondering how my family was connected to the head of the Scottish vampire clan. I was curious too—it was something I would be asking my mother about when I saw her.

"So then, Marcus, let's hear what's brought you up to my neck of the woods and got you hiding a beautiful woman in a vampire hold," asked Alabaster, turning his attention to his next victim.

Marcus shrugged. "Council investigation." Alabaster did not look satisfied with that answer. Marcus sighed and carried on, seeing he wasn't going to get out of this one. "It's the mortal drug that keeps popping up. We're going to see if the Oracle has any insight into the larger picture."

Alabaster looked surprised at this. "Are you now… well, isn't that interesting?" he said, looking over at me with a knowing glance.

I sipped my drink without comment, ignoring his curious look. I was tempted to stick my tongue out at him, but thought that might amuse him too.

"What's a vampire hold?" I asked, trying to steer the conversation anywhere else but talk of the Oracle.

"Vampires, like the soulless, aren't overly welcome in most lodgings, so the vampires have a network of properties that can be used as a temporary lodging for our kind in most major cities and a few of the more popular out of the way places," Marcus answered, glad to move away from talk of the investigation. He thought for a moment before giving me a sly smile and turning his attention to Alabaster. "Holds are for out-of-town visitors, which makes a person wonder what you're doing here, Alabaster… last I heard, you lived here in Inverness." Alabaster looked guilty.

"Ah, you caught me! I'm hiding from my wife, Maggie." He got up for another drink. "Every spring, she gets it into her head to renovate the entire house and change everything. It's those damn shows on the telly she watches that do it. I dun like to paint, and I cannot tell rosewater pink for dusty sunset pink."

I choked on a sip of my drink, coughing before letting go of a laugh. This powerful head of a vampire clan had been run out of the house by his wife's renovations. That was too much for my tired brain to process.

"I had a meeting with the other clan heads tonight, and I'm just taking my time getting back, is all," he said, looking sheepish.

Marcus perked up at the mention of a clan meeting. "That's strange. That's the third one this month."

Alabaster turned serious again, coming to stand in front of the fireplace. His face looked older somehow in the firelight. "These are strange times. You'd do well to pay more attention to clan business, lad; you won't be able to gallivant around playing investigator for much longer. At some point, Prince Alexander will come a-calling for you, whether or not you like it."

Marcus looked away, annoyance all over his features. I got the sense this was a long-standing disagreement between the two of them. I wondered what he meant by his comment. The current vampire queen had only come to power in the last fifty years or so, relatively recently by vampire standards. She had appointed her son, Prince Alexander, to be the next head of the soulless army, being a soulless himself. He was not eligible for the throne, but he still wielded considerable power. If the gossip was to be believed, he was both dangerous and secretive, declining to attend most public functions or vampire political gatherings.

Alabaster carried on, ignoring Marcus's look of disdain. "Several older vampires have been found murdered in recent weeks, and it appears to have been done by a cell of the Human First movement. What once thought of as a fringe group in America seems to have migrated and gathered strength here in the UK. It's spreading at an alarming rate, and we can not pin down the hows and whos of it no matter how we try." He sighed, turning to sit in the chair once more.

That was a lot to take in. Murdering a vampire was no simple task, and the older they were, the more powerful they tended to be. How had humans done this—not just once, but repeatedly? It spoke of more than just a passing movement of unrest happening in isolation. It was unsettling. I watched the fire dance as my eyes got heavy, losing track of the conversation between Marcus and Alabaster. The noise had become a comforting hum of company that was lulling me to sleep.

"Alena."

Hearing my name, I snapped awake. Alabaster was looking at me with concern in his eyes.

"Go to bed, lass, you're dead on your feet. The rooms are made up, top of the stairs to the right," he said. I looked over at Marcus, wondering if he was going to bed as well, but he seemed lost in thought, giving me a slight nod of goodnight. I got up from my cozy spot by the fire and headed up the stairs, grabbing my bags along the way. I paused halfway up; my bag was slipping from my arm and needed readjustment. Below me, I heard Alabaster and Marcus continue talking.

"Smart lass you've found there." Marcus hummed in agreement, lost in his own thoughts. Alabaster's tone turned serious. "She's a witch, though, if I'm not mistaken, and a powerful one at that—you'd best tread carefully." He put his empty whisky glass down on the table with a clink, moving to poke the dying fire. "You cannot avoid fate forever, Marcus, as much as you'd like to. Someday you will be bound to another soulless. It's the way of things. You need to stop running from your responsibilities."

Marcus did not reply, and just sat silently watching the fire. I figured I was finished eavesdropping for the evening. I wondered what responsibilities Marcus was avoiding. Did he already have a bound mate? Why did Alabaster think I was powerful? That was absurd. I could grow a pretty mean cactus, but that was where my power ended. These were problems for a more rested brain; my head was spinning with everything I had learned this evening. I crept silently up the rest of the stairs to find my bed, though I doubted I would have a restful night.

Chapter 17

"I should probably drive from here," I said as we approached the familiar laneway. The drive from Inverness had been quiet, and Marcus had been monosyllabic all morning. I wondered what else had been discussed last night that had left him in such a pensive mood. I worried that something else was going on other than just escalating unrest amongst the humans.

Marcus pulled over slowly to the side of the tree-lined lane, sliding out of the driver's seat without a word. As we met behind the car, he pulled me in for a quick kiss.

"Stop worrying. I'll end up with holes in the side of my head if you keep staring at me like that."

I opened my mouth to deny it, but he carried on before I could get a word out.

"I can literally hear you thinking. You're a loud thinker, and your eyebrows crease when you're worried." He made a ridiculous frowning face while tapping me on the forehead, mocking me.

If he was okay enough to be making fun of me, it couldn't be that bad. I let some worries from the morning slip away. If he was mixed up with the vampire royals and their complicated politics, he would tell me when he was ready.

"It's just asinine vampire nonsense—promise," he said. I still doubted it was just that, but I let it go. Today was going to be stressful enough for me without adding fresh problems on top of existing concerns. I was intensely nervous about our meeting with the Oracle.

"I'm going on faith here. You're not going to drive us over a cliff, okay," he said, handing me the keys.

"Sir, I am offended!" I said mockingly. I took the wheel and guided us back onto the narrow road.

"You want to fill me in on where we're going yet?" he asked for the third or tenth time on the drive. I had lost track a while ago.

"I told you, we're going to meet the Oracle," I said again, sighing. "Look, it's complicated, okay?" I relented, trying to pacify his grumpy demeanour at my non-answer. I turned onto what looked like an abandoned dirt track. The Range Rover was struggling a little, and I had to focus on navigating the dips and large potholes.

After a little way, I sensed the wards protecting the house. I slowed down and took Marcus's hand in mine so they would recognize him as being my guest. The wards were serious business. They would fry anyone who was not family, or an invited guest. He squeezed my hand as the tingling wards washed over us. We drove slowly around the bend and saw the sturdy stone cottage.

"We're here." I announced and jumped out of the truck. Breathing the clean, cold air made all the dark thoughts and concerns I had been harbouring these past few weeks fall away, and I felt lighter than I had in a while. I was home. It had been close to a year since I had last been here. I vowed silently to myself to return more often in the future.

Marcus was looking around the meadow with some scepticism. I tried to see it through his eyes. The cottage was large but haphazardly built, as if the additions had been constructed as afterthoughts, which, in reality, they had been: the place had a mind of its own, adding and subtracting rooms on whims known only to itself. There were children's toys flung carelessly around the lawn and I noticed as we approached the wooden fence that it had in parts fallen down. Something that may have been a gate at one point was propped up against a pole.

Without warning, there was a loud pop and a small boy of about ten appeared in front of us.

"Len! You're late!" he said sternly, his dark eyes glittering. "I'm hungry. Mum is making pancakes." And with another loud pop, he was gone.

I laughed and carried on up toward the house. Marcus looked over at me, no doubt about to ask what madness he had walked into, when, with another ear-splitting pop, the boy was back, shoving his dark black hair out of his eyes.

"Oh, Mum says to leave the stuff in the car. She made the cottage up for you and your boyfriend," he said. "Lenny Has A Boyfriend." He mocked me in a singsong voice while making kissy faces. Before I could grab him, he popped away again. That little shit. I was totally going to get him back for this.

"Lenny?" Marcus asked, looking delighted at the nickname. Without acknowledging him, I pushed open the cottage's wide Dutch door with a grunt.

It took me a moment to adjust to the dimmer interior after the bright sunlight outside. I took off my shoes and motioned for Marcus to do the same. The hallway was jammed with coats, toys, and various footwear. As I tried to find a place to stash my boots, a loud voice yelled from the kitchen.

"Ay, put them anywhere—the mess won't care." I dropped them beside some books on the floor and headed toward the sounds of life from within the cottage.

I navigated the large, crowded, open space serving as living room, dining room, playroom, and office in equal parts, finally reaching my destination. Before I could plunk down at the kitchen counter, a small woman appeared and wrapped me in a warm hug.

"It's about time you made it home," she said.

I melted into her embrace. "Hi, Mum."

Marcus's eyebrows crept higher and higher on his forehead as he watched this exchange until I was sure they would fall off the other side. I turned to him.

"Marcus, this is Celeste MacKenzie, also The Oracle, and my mum."

Marcus inclined his head. "An honour to meet you," he said before sitting down; I could see his mind was finally putting all the pieces together. His expression revealed his dawning understanding.

"Oh, enough of that honour nonsense—I get enough of that when I get dragged to council meetings. I take it Alena failed to mention I was her mum, eh?" She shot me a disapproving look. "Yeah, that sounds like something you would do."

I cringed. Okay, maybe it was uncalled for. It had seemed like a good idea at the time. I didn't like being known as the Oracle's daughter. The title came with many expectations and assumptions that I didn't want. I wanted to make my life based on my own accomplishments. I perched on the stool next to Marcus. She put cups of tea in front of Marcus and me and went back to the stove to prepare our late breakfast.

Upstairs there was a pop followed by a loud crash.

"Connor!" she yelled. "No teleporting in the house! Get down here and set the table."

"He's getting better, but his aim still needs some work—preferably not in here," she said to us absently.

Connor, looking suitably chastened, thumped down the steps, followed by what could have been a younger version of Celeste. The little girl, about three, stomped up to her dramatically.

"Hi Lenny," she said.

I scooped my little sister up into my lap, kissing the top of her dark, curly hair.

"Mumma, I don't want peas for dinner!" she whined.

I tried and failed to hide my giggling. Celeste shot me a look that said I should probably stop laughing, or she would be after me next. I put the wiggling Molly down on the floor.

Crouching in front of her youngest daughter, Celeste brushed her messy hair out of her face and patiently asked, "Now Molly, what have I told you about looking into the future for personal reasons?"

Molly kicked her foot at the floor and looked down. "Not to," she answered softly.

Celeste carried on. "And why not?"

Molly answered reluctantly. "Because stuff might not be true," she sighed. "But Mum, I hate peas!" Molly pleaded.

"Go wash your hands for breakfast," she said, and Molly stomped off again.

"Ugh, a toddler who can see the future is bloody aggravating!" Celeste declared, throwing up her hands dramatically.

Marcus had watched the entire exchange with a bemused expression.

Celeste declared it time to eat and wrangled the lot of us toward a massive oak table. The space was clearly being used as a dining room but may have lived a previous life as a greenhouse: it was graced with floor-to-ceiling windows with plants haphazardly mounted to the large timbers holding the whole structure up. I sat down at the table, joined by Marcus in the chair beside me. Glancing at him quickly, I saw he was taking this all in his stride, though this house wasn't done with its surprises.

I watched him as I asked my mother, "Where is Will?"

Celeste sighed dramatically, bringing the remaining dishes to the table.

"Probably in the workshop." She turned to Connor. "Go fetch your da."

Connor set down the pile of mismatched cutlery on the table and disappeared with a pop.

"William MacKenzie? As in the inventor?" Marcus asked excitedly, his eyes lighting up.

Yup, there it was. It was terrible being the daughter of the Oracle. Still, it could not match the aggravation of being the daughter of William MacKenzie. Despite this, I loved Will with all my heart. He had met Mum when I was ten. I was never quite clear how the romance had happened, but he had slid into our lives as if he had always belonged there. His soft-spoken demeanour and calm presence through the turmoil of adolescence had been the balance to my mother's brash and vocal nature.

Marcus was going to go full-on fanboy all over Will. I could see it all now. I had seen that look many times before, I thought, sighing inwardly: it had been a recurring theme with my friends throughout secondary school. They would come over to study or watch a movie and, without fail, would end up in Will's workshop looking at his latest creation. Will had achieved fame for his shielding charms, which enabled magic users to use modern technology without destroying them. Magic and modern technology had never mixed well, and he was the man who opened the world of smartphones and social media to a generation of magical teenagers. It was like living with one of the Beatles.

"Yes, he is that William MacKenzie," I said.

Celeste gave my shoulder a commiserating squeeze, knowing the look on Marcus's face as well. Marcus grinned back at me.

Connor's excited chatter and Will's softer male voice floated in from the kitchen before the two appeared in the doorway. Will was carrying Connor, who was a miniature version of him. They shared the dark, messy hair and large, dark eyes. He nodded hello, dropping a quick kiss on my head as he passed behind the chair and settling himself and Connor at the table beside Marcus. With the rest of the MacKenzie brood finally at the table, breakfast started in earnest. I watched as Marcus peppered Will with questions, while Molly regaled me with gossip about her doll's adventures.

As Will cleared the plates, and the kids escaped to the bowels of the house, Celeste turned her regard to us.

"So, you need me to help with your investigation?" She directed the question at Marcus.

"Yes, we've hit a dead-end, and I think there's something bigger going on that could affect us all."

"Hmmm. Well, I'm not sure how much help I could be, but we can have a go." She looked at me with a mischievous grin. "I will need supplies, though," she said, looking at me.

Oh no, not this again. I hated going to the woods for supplies.

"Sure, whatever you need," Marcus agreed quickly, unaware of what he was signing us up for.

She smiled knowingly at me and reached for her premade list, placing it on the table. She'd clearly been planning this. I snatched the list off the table and flopped back in my chair.

"Muuuum," I whined, suddenly feeling like a petulant child given an unpleasant chore.

She rose from the table, grabbing the remaining dishes as she went.

"They like you," she said, laughing. "It's not that bad, and it's not as if I can go. Be back by sunset, and we'll cast the circle then," she said, heading toward the kitchen. "Have fun!" she yelled over her shoulder, still chuckling happily to herself.

I grumped, looking at the list again. The woods were enchanted, so they stayed moderately warm and green year-round. The issue was the occupants of the woods. Brownies. Usually, brownies lived in houses, but these had declared independence from the trappings of human dwellings centuries ago and since then had occupied the woods south of the cottage. They were bossy, nosy, frustrating creatures with no sense of personal space. They treated me well enough most of the time, but enjoyed playing tricks on me or hiding the personal items I brought to the woods when searching for herbs and mushrooms for my mother.

Mum and the brownies had been feuding for as long as I could remember; neither side would admit fault, and I think they had forgotten why they had started in the first place. Either Will or I were always chosen as the supply gatherer, since they wouldn't drive us out with pointy sticks and rocks like they would her.

Marcus looked at me for direction. "So, supplies?" he asked.

He's probably wondering why I was pouting like a child in my chair. I grumbled to myself some more before standing. Might as well get this over with.

"Come on," I said.

Manoeuvring through the house, Marcus close on my heels, I grabbed a satchel from the pegs on the wall and headed out the front door. I really hoped I would get through this without having my phone and bra stolen again.

Chapter 18

I stomped down the path toward the SUV, jerking open the door and muttering under my breath in Gaelic about the unfairness of the task. I switched to French, then English, when I ran out of swear words I knew in those languages. Marcus regarded me the way you would a hangry toddler: with caution, sympathy, and a great degree of humour.

"What?" I asked him as I chucked my watch, phone, and keys on the passenger seat.

"Are you going to enlighten me as to what we've just signed up for? Clearly, it's going to be unpleasant by the way you're cursing in at least three different languages." He didn't look concerned about a mystery mission. If anything, he looked excited about the prospect of traipsing off into unknown danger.

I sighed audibly. It wasn't going to be that bad. Probably.

"We're going to the woods to fetch some herbs and plants for Celeste." I paused, trying to find the right words. "The woods are occupied by a tribe of brownies." On paper, that didn't sound so bad. In reality, though, it was highly aggravating.

"That's all? That doesn't sound so terrible." he said confidently. He picked up my satchel and headed toward the gravel path that led to the distant line of trees.

I took in his outfit: black slacks with a black sweater. It looked good on him. I willed myself to focus on the task at hand. "You may want to change into something a little less… I don't know, nice?" I called after him, hoping this time he would take my advice. The last time he ignored my warnings, it had cost him his shoes. Every time I ventured into the woods, I came back grass stained, torn up, and muddy. He just waved away my suggestion. It seemed Marcus was a slow learner. Well then, I supposed if he came back in tatters, it would be on him.

I jogged to catch up with him. "You'll see what I mean soon enough," I huffed.

As we approached the forest's perimeter, the air grew warmer, and the gravel path changed to dusty dirt. I paused at what I had come to understand was the boundary between Celeste's land and that of the brownies. I sat on the mossy rock that marked the path into the heart of the wood and removed my shoes and socks. Marcus watched me intently.

"Do you like your shoes?" I asked.

Marcus looked down at the fancy black loafers. "I'd like to keep them if that's what you're implying." He eyed me suspiciously. "I seem to lose shoes rather quickly around you, though."

"I'm not implying anything, just strongly recommending that you may not want to take anything in there you aren't willing to lose," I said, wiggling my toes in the warm breeze. I never liked shoes. Too restrictive. I waited. When it was clear Marcus was going to ignore my warning again, I got up and led the way down the worn path.

The air became warmer and more humid the further we went. I stripped out of my light sweater and hung it on a branch, hoping it would still be there when we passed this way on our journey out. Marcus gave me a wolfish grin as he took in my tight tank top with its hot pink bra peeking out the side. I shoved him lightly on the shoulder.

"Quit staring," I said, though I didn't mean it at all.

He grabbed for me when I went to shove him again and quickly lowered his lips to mine, kissing me thoroughly. I stumbled back a bit, going up on my tiptoes to delve deeper into the kiss.

Above me, I heard a singsong voice chant, "Alena and a soulless kissing in a tree... K-I-S-S-I-N-G."

"What the hell?" Marcus looked up into the tree, trying to locate the voice.

I chuckled. "Snickerdoodle! Knock it off," I said in the direction of the growing laughter above us. I would recognize that obnoxious little troublemaker's voice anywhere. I didn't bother to look up. Unless the brownies wanted to be seen, you wouldn't find them.

"Snickerdoodle?" Marcus asked as he laughed at the brownie's ridiculous name.

I waved my hands, motioning frantically at him to stop laughing, but it was too late. Snickerdoodle had leapt down from the tree onto Marcus's shoulder and grabbed him roughly by the ear.

"Are you laughing at my name, soulless? Eh? My ma gave me that name, and she was a right fine lady! She gave me a good and proper name too! Don't you be starting nothing! These here are my woods—none be making fun of me here," he screeched loudly.

Marcus finally snagged the flailing little man off his shoulder and held him up by the back of his shirt. The tiny creature tried in vain to look threatening, swinging his tiny fists around and squeaking creative curses at Marcus.

"Hello, Snickerdoodle," he said, taking in the brownie's appearance. Only six inches high, his wide-set eyes were slightly too large for his face and his paper-thin skin had a slight green tinge to it. He was dressed in a mishmash of patchwork fabrics decorated with small rocks and colourful beads. Snickerdoodle gave up his angry rant and hung limply with his arms crossed, looking sullen.

"Put me down, you big lump—show some respect for your elders!" he huffed, taking an idle kick at Marcus's nose.

Marcus put him down gently on the path, and Snickerdoodle took off, vanishing into a nearby bush.

"Well, that was interesting," he said, absently looking around the woods for more tiny short-tempered brownies to fall from the trees.

"Alena, you're home!" came a shrill voice from nearby. Happier chitters joined the first on the long branch above my head. Before long, six tiny brownies had materialized out of the dense leaves and crowded onto the narrow space to look down at us. The one who had called out my name stepped gracefully onto my outstretched hand, and I held her up to my face.

"Tenderfoot, good to see you," I said, nodding respectfully, and I meant it. Tenderfoot was the tribe leader and was less mischievous than the rest. Or at least she never got caught stealing things out of my bag when I wasn't looking. Either way, the other brownies tended to be less rambunctious when she was supervising them.

While I had been saying my hellos, the other brownies had crept over to Marcus and were scrutinizing him. Questions erupted from the crowd of tiny people.

"You brought us a soulless?"

"I've never seen a soulless before. Do they bite?"

"Oh, look, these are so fancy," one cried as he undid the shoelaces and, with deft little fingers, pulled them off the shoes.

"He's a looker, Alena, can we keep him?" asked one plump brownie.

"What's under all this," she said, climbing under the hem of his shirt. "Oh my, oh my, indeed."

"Alena, have you seen this? It's yummy." She peeked her head out from the shirt and disappeared again before Marcus could grab her. Her head popped out once more. "I approve. Oh, what's in his pants?" she winked at me before scrambling back under his shirt.

I watched, trying to contain my laughter. It was awful to be the one they were harassing, but watching someone else be the subject of their keen curiosity was vastly entertaining. Marcus looked at me pleadingly. He clearly didn't want to hurt them, looking to me to save him from the intimate inspection and barrage of invasive questions.

The brownie popped out the bottom of Marcus's sweater and reached for his belt buckle. With quick motions, she had it undone and had taken it off before he could react. Marcus finally grabbed her before she could undress him any further, setting her gently on the grass. She skittered away with her stolen belt into the woods, cackling happily. Unable to contain myself any longer, I laughed, watching him trying to pull the curious brownies off his clothing.

"I got his keys!" one shrieked. The jangle of keys and merry laughter disappeared into the woods.

"Hey! I need those!" he cried angrily.

He watched, helpless to fend them off, as they systematically robbed him of everything he had brought with him. I watched his shoelaces disappear under a rock and shrugged at him.

"I told you to leave everything behind," I said.

I placed Tenderfoot on my shoulder and started down the path, leaving Marcus to fend off the tiny creatures. He didn't listen to me, so I'll let him figure it out, I thought. He wasn't in any danger, though his dignity and pride might be a tad bruised by the time they were done with him. Leaving the angry shouts and peels of shrieking laughter behind me, I headed to the heart of the woods with Tenderfoot.

"Celeste sent you for supplies?" she asked.

I nodded, handing her the list.

"That's odd, is it not? I thought she had stopped using her powers," she said, more to herself than to me.

I too had wondered why she had agreed so readily to do this for us. Celeste was old. I was never sure how old, since she told no one, but I knew her powers were waning. It was the natural order of things that Molly was now coming into her powers; they would slowly siphon off Celeste and transfer to her. I knew using her powers now was growing more difficult for her.

"It is strange," I agreed, but didn't elaborate. It had been a thought rumbling in the back of my mind since we arrived. I trusted Celeste to know what she was doing, but she was still my mum, so it was impossible not to worry.

"Most of this will be found by the lake." Tenderfoot said, pointing toward the small body of water hidden behind some willow trees.

An angry roar reached us from where we had left the others. I looked back, wondering if I should go rescue Marcus.

Tenderfoot chuckled. "I should go rescue your friend from the others. Take care, Alena. Change is coming; I can feel it on the wind. Stay safe." Without another word, she dropped off my shoulder, moving swiftly back the way we had come.

I sat on a nearby log and waited for Marcus to catch up. Pondering Tenderfoot's words, I felt it too. Changes were coming, but I wondered if it would be good. I was finding it hard to be optimistic.

Chapter 19

A bedraggled and annoyed-looking Marcus rounded the bend, stomping angrily over to where I sat. I tried not to grin, but it was impossible. He had utterly nailed the dishevelled and sexy look. It was hard not to enjoy it. He sat down beside me, hanging his head, clearly defeated. I chuckled because it was hilarious that a powerful soulless had been dominated by a handful of tiny, mostly harmless, brownies. Marcus shot me a look of pure scorn that set me off. I howled with laughter. Before long, I was on the ground giggling hard enough my stomach was aching. Marcus didn't look impressed as he dusted off his pants and wiggled his shoeless feet in the dirt, which only made me laugh harder. Before long, I heard him chuckle, too.

"They are so horrid!" he complained. "They stole my belt and my shoes! I loved those shoes." He looked down at his bare feet again. "I seem to have an issue maintaining my footwear since meeting you," he lamented.

"I told you!" I said, wiping the tears from my eyes. Getting up, I helped Marcus up off the log.

"Come on, let's get what we need and get out of here before you lose your pants," I said, winking at him suggestively. I really wouldn't have minded him losing those too much.

Marcus sighed dramatically before joining me on the path, picking his way gently, trying not to step on sharp pebbles. I led him down the gentle slope that opened up to reveal a small lake. The water sparkled in the sun as if it was made of diamonds.

"It's beautiful," Marcus said, breathing out slowly, taking it all in.

We worked our way down around the lake. I pointed out which plants to pick. Before long, we had everything we needed. The sun had moved past midday and had started its descent toward the horizon. I lay down on the grass, taking a break from digging in the dirt. Looking up at the blue sky, I relaxed, letting my thoughts float away with the wispy clouds overhead. Marcus lay down beside me without a word.

"As the daughter of the Oracle, should you not share her powers?" he asked out of the blue.

I rolled over to face him. He looked like he was trying to fit all the pieces together, as if everything he had learned about my family in the past few days was a puzzle that needed solving. I sighed. I wasn't a fan of digging up the past for inspection, but I supposed it was a valid question. I rolled back over.

"Celeste adopted me when I was eight," I replied, wondering how much of this story I wanted to share with him. It was an ugly story for such a beautiful afternoon. "She had a vision of me being alone and scared. It took her a while to find me, but she did, eventually."

I shuddered, remembering the time before that moment. I had spent nearly six months on the streets of London, trying to survive after my birth mother had abandoned me. My mother was human; I recalled very little about her, and none of it was pleasant, but the day she left me on the sidewalk was burned into my mind with unyielding clarity. Her visceral hatred of anything to do with magic had turned on me with full force that day. I remember her fists connecting with my small chest over and over as I cried for her to stop, too small to fight back. Her screaming was a rage-filled rant. Her shrill screeching detailed how I was a vile abomination. It still echoed through my nightmares. I shuddered in a breath, letting the memories wash over me.

"She saved my life. Mum legally adopted me a year after bringing me here. So she is my mum in every sense of the word, but Molly gets her powers." I was glad to have avoided inheriting Celeste's powers; I had watched over the years how they weighed on her. When I thought of Molly having to take this on, it made me profoundly unhappy. I wish I could save her from it. Molly was full of life, and the Oracle's path was a burden that I hoped would not extinguish that light. I had learned early that life was cruel, and I wanted to spare Molly from that for as long as possible.

Marcus pondered what I had told him. He sat up, taking in my dispirited face. He lowered slowly until his face was inches from mine. I met his gaze, my memories of the past overshadowed by his closeness, helping to drive my mind away from the lingering sorrow. He slid his hand slowly up my ribs in a soothing caress.

"I'm sorry, I didn't mean to poke at painful memories." He slid his hand under my shirt, his warm caress sending shivers up my spine. "Every time I think I have you figured out, I learn something else, and I have to fit it all back together again." He ran a thumb along the underside of my bra. "What other secrets are you hiding, I wonder?"

The warm sunlight and his light touch were making me

dizzy. I pulled him down toward me, lazily wrapping my arms around his neck, eager to banish the past and enjoy this moment. He kissed me lightly, but what had started out as a passive comfort was quickly stoking the fires of desire. Soft touches become demanding. He had unsnapped my bra and palmed one of my small breasts, tugging on the hard nipple as I demanded more from his tongue. He groaned into my hair as I ground against him. A soft snicker from the nearby copse of trees gave Marcus pause.

"We aren't alone, are we?" he whispered.

"No, we absolutely are not." I agreed, trying to decide if I cared about having an audience. Looking up into the trees, I saw Snickerdoodle waving and winking ridiculously. Well, that was a bit of a mood killer.

"It's time to get back anyway," I said reluctantly.

He sighed, disappointment and frustration in his voice. "I really dislike these brownies of yours," he said, untangling himself from me and helping me to my feet. I couldn't help but agree. I adjusted my clothing and grabbed the satchel of plants. It was time to head back now, anyway.

As we headed up the hill toward the path, loud shouts followed us.

"Awww, come on."

"We won't judge."

"Just pretend we aren't here!"

I laughed. "Those little shits."

Marcus grinned back at me as the teasing grew more elaborate and ridiculous. "I really, really don't like them," he shouted.

"Respect your elders, you big soulless oaf!" A jingle and a rustling of leaves was all the warning he got before his car keys came sailing out of the tree and hit him square in the back of the head.

"Hey!" he rubbed the spot where the projectile had connected and scooped up the keys off the grass. A chorus of snickering erupted from the nearby trees.

"Let's go before they cause us more trouble," I said, taking his hand. We headed up the path away from the lake. By the time we reached the cottage with our hard-won prizes, the sun was setting. Celeste appeared in the doorway as we approached.

"Have a delightful afternoon?" she asked sweetly, taking in Marcus's unkempt appearance.

Marcus did not look amused. "Your neighbours are thieving and perverse little creatures," he said grumpily.

She was digging through our spoils and not paying attention. "Oh, that's nice, dear," she said and wandered away with her prizes, still picking through the basket.

I shrugged. Celeste was used to our loud and vigorous complaining about the brownies. It just washed over her now.

We headed into the house, following the delicious smells of dinner wafting from the dining room. Will and the kids had already started without us. We took our seats and served ourselves before while Celeste wandered in from the kitchen.

"Good work. Looks like everything's there," she said, taking a seat at the table.

"Brownie duty?" Will asked.

"Suckers," Connor snickered between mouthfuls of potatoes. "Did they take your bra again? You know they have a tree full of them on the far side near the lake."

Molly chimed in, "I like the pink sparkly one."

To avoid being teased further by my loving and supportive family, I turned to my mother, attempting to ignore the faces

Connor and Molly were making at me. Marcus was laughing softly under his breath at my sibling's shenanigans, being of no help whatsoever.

"We ran into an old vampire named Alabaster in Inverness," I said, watching for a reaction. My mum had always been cagey on details of her exploits before I showed up. I was forever trying to pry stories of her adventures out of her and Will.

To my surprise, it was Will who answered me.

"That old troublemaker is still alive? I would have thought Maggie would have buried him on the moors by now."

"Troublemaker indeed," she huffed. "And what did he have to say for himself?"

"Not much. He wanted to know where you were and sends his regards. He asked if you would visit him and Maggie soon." I glanced over at Will to find him listening intently. "He also said he had something of yours you may want back?" I said, directing the comment to Celeste.

"Hmm, I see," she said, giving Will a meaningful glance. "Perhaps we'll make a trip down to see the old crudmuffin." She turned her attention to the children, quizzing them on what they had gotten up to in school that day, effectively ending the conversation.

I chanced a questioning glance at Will, wondering if he would add something to appease my curiosity. When he noticed my attention, he just shook his head subtly, an apologetic look crossing his face. Well, damn, I guess my life was going to have to endure some more mystery too. I hated mysteries. I sat back, full of more food than was probably wise to have eaten. My mum was a prolific cook. There was always ten times more food than we could actually eat. I smiled at the loud and chaotic scene that was dinner. It was good to be home.

"Come on, little ones, time for a bath and bed," Will announced.

Molly and Connor had looked like they were going to make a break for it, hoping to avoid bedtime just a little longer. "Nooo," they cried in unison.

They allowed themselves to be marched up the stairs by Will, looking like they were off to face some horrible but inevitable demise.. Celeste vanished into her workroom to prepare for casting the circle later this evening, leaving Marcus and me to clear up.

The ordinary domestic routine of dinner and dishes was comforting. I was taken aback at how well Marcus slid into my life with ease. He spoke to the kids with ease that conveyed experience and held his own against my mother's not-so-subtle interrogation. I felt an ache in my chest at the thought of the hole he would leave in my life when he eventually moved on. It was so easy to forget there was no romantic happily ever-after in the future for us. I wiped the last of the dishes off and piled them away in the cupboards.

Celeste appeared in the kitchen with a solemn-looking Will by her side.

"It's time."

Chapter 20

We gathered around the stone-paved firepit that was set away from the cottage down a gentle slope. The crash of waves on the distant beach below was the only sound on the murky night. I shivered in the damp spring air, apprehensive about what we were about to undertake. I had watched my mother do this numerous times in the past, but tonight, it felt ominous. Will stood by like a silent sentinel, the gloom of the night making him appear more shadow than man. Celeste started her preparations, setting the ward stones in her usual business-like manner. Marcus watched with interest. She used salt to draw an elaborate circle and symbols on the smooth stone surface. Having seen this several times before, I knew where my place would be. I moved to the spot inside the circle across from Celeste. I motioned for Marcus to stand by my side.

Celeste took her place when the circle was finished, throwing a mixture of herbs on the fire. The flames sputtered for a moment before bursting up and changing to a blinding white fire. Celeste raised her hands, dragging a dense mist from the ground at our feet. As the fire settled down, an ethereal chanting started and mist rose around us. The voice of billions of years of humanity was a low hum that grew to a deafening pandemonium before the mists rose from the ground to meet above our heads, cutting the din off abruptly. The silence was complete in the sphere that surrounded us. All that remained of the Highlands was the paved stone circle we stood on.

Mum had tried to explain the process to me when I was a child. The Oracle's power lets her strip away the visible reality, showing her the entirety of space and time at once. Time and space, she explained, were one and the same. I had never really understood the ins and outs of it. She always lost me around the point when she started in on the quantum mechanics of it. The closest I had ever come to comprehension was when, in an exasperated rant of frustration, she had said it was "like a big ball of wibbly-wobbly, timey-wimey stuff," quoting a more articulate time traveller than herself. She used the threads of possibilities to navigate, following them to find answers in the past, present and future.

Every time I saw her power used, it left me in awe. I watched as the metallic filaments created delicate webs that crackled and flash around us. The thin lines that represented all the possibilities of every choice for every person rose around us. Celeste opened her eyes, which had turned a milky white. She moved her hands in nimble and gentle waves, directing the threads around as they spun in the mist. The hypnotic beauty of her movements left me entranced.

The spell was broken by a sudden shudder under my feet. The delicate mist around us cracked with bolts of sharp blue lightning before churning angrily and losing its sphere shape. The mist dissipated quickly as the cold highland night took shape around us once more. That was not normal. I watched in horror as Celeste collapsed bonelessly down in the Adirondack chair behind her. Will crouched in front of her, looking concerned but unsurprised.

"I'm fine, I'm fine," she said. She waved him off weakly.

He draped a blanket over her as she shivered. I looked on, alarmed. I'd never see her like this before. Tired, yes, but this was extreme. I would never have asked this of her had I known how much it would drain her. Will looked back at us unhappily. He scooped her up despite her protests and swept her into the house. I followed them inside. Marcus stayed outside. I imagined he sensed this was something for our family to address in privacy.

I sat on the floor beside the sofa where Will had laid Celeste out, covering her with an erratically coloured afghan.

"Mum, why didn't you say something?" I said softly, hurt bleeding through my voice.

Will snorted. "Because she's stubborn—sound familiar?" he said, giving us both a look of tired exasperation. He stood. "I'll let you two talk." He shot Celeste a meaningful look.

She sighed, leaning back on the sofa and pulling the afghan around her shoulders. I wanted her to say something, but she just sat there silently, looking at nothing. Frustrated, I got up to leave. No one forced Celeste MacKenzie to do anything she didn't want to do. If she wanted to sulk, I'd leave her to it.

"Alena, sit your butt down!" she said to my back.

I sat back down across from her. I wanted to fight and yell, but she looked so sunken and small lying there I couldn't bring myself to be angry with her. This was my fault; I should never have asked this of her. I plopped back down on the floor, leaning my head on the sofa. Mum started stroking my hair absently, looking at the fire with a faraway look on her face.

"We've talked about this before, you know, when Molly was born." She sounded tired. We had talked about it, but that was then. Being faced with the reality now was not the same thing at all. I thought we would have more time. Molly was still a baby.

"It's the way things are, and despite what everyone seems to think, this process, while unpleasant, will not kill me. I even look forward to losing my powers. They aren't actually a bucket of laughs, you know."

She sat up slightly to look at me. "I'll remind you as well that Will has a mortal lifetime. I want to age and experience all that with him. The wrinkles, the backaches, the forgetfulness—all of it. It means giving up immortality, sure, but would you want to live forever, knowing you would have to watch everyone you love pass on without you?"

I shrugged; I had never given it much thought before, though I understood what she was saying. I was still not happy about this situation. I didn't like the idea of losing her ever. As a child, I had always assumed she would live forever. She was this mystical creature full of power, never changing, timeless. The thought had brought me comfort: at least this one person was forever. I was never in danger of being abandoned again. Now it seemed even that was going to change. As an adult, I could see what she said made sense—even agree with her—but my child's heart ached at the thought of more loss.

"Enough of this," she said dismissively. "Let's talk about what I found, which sadly wasn't much, and it wasn't good. You remember I can't see much of your path?"

I nodded. I did recall that. It made sense in a way that she could not see the past or future of those closest to her. It was a protective measure ingrained in her magic. Her magic hid these things from her, or she could drive herself mad with worry, seeing all the possibilities for people she loved.

"Because it seems your path is so interwoven with this investigation and the consequences of the outcome, it was hard to unravel it all." She sighed, clearly frustrated. "I have little to help you, though the drugs you keep finding are a part of a larger story than I think we all had assumed."

"And the bodies on my lawn?" I asked.

"No idea. So far as I can tell, nothing is connecting them to the drugs at all." She looked thoughtful for a moment. "Are you sure they're connected?"

"Pretty sure."

"Hmm, well, that's all I got regarding the investigation. I don't have the strength to look too much deeper."

"It's fine, Mum."

"I found something else, though. As I was picking apart the threads between you and Marcus, something is joining you that even I don't understand. No matter how I tried, I couldn't pull them apart. It bears consideration. I think Marcus is good for you, but he's also involved in something dangerous—which makes him dangerous." She said, running her hands through her long white hair.

"Please be careful," she said as her eyes drifted closed. I tucked the blanket around her and pulled down another one on top of her, hoping she would warm up. Her face was still so pale. I looked down at her once more before leaving the room, heading out to where Will and Marcus were seated around the dying fire.

"Everything okay?" Marcus asked when I appeared at the fire pit.

I nodded, slumping into an empty chair. "Mum is sleeping," I said.

Will rose smoothly and ghosted back into the house to be

close to her. They were always like that. Never apart for long, even in the same house. Marcus had been strangely quiet through the entire event, observing everyone closely but not commenting. He sat watching the embers pensively, then looked up at me as I yawned absentmindedly.

"You okay?" he said.

"Yeah, just tired. Come on, let's go down to the cottage and get settled. I need to sleep, and it's getting cold out here." I said, heading for the car to grab my bags. He took everything from my tired arms and followed me down the narrow path to the guest cottage on the cliff side. It was within sight of the main house but far enough away to give privacy. The little cottage had been built years after the main house; it had a more modern aesthetic with large windows and copper accents. As we approached, Marcus cleared his throat awkwardly.

"Did she see anything that could help?" he asked. I was surprised he had repressed his questions for this long. I was grateful for the slight reprieve as I tried to sort through everything in my head.

"Yeah, but nothing that would be helpful, I don't think." I dumped my stuff just outside the main door of the cottage and flopped down on the bench outside, overlooking the sea. The breeze was chilly here, but not unpleasantly so, and we were sheltered by a small ridge. Marcus sat down beside me, watching the waves.

"She said there was no connection between the bodies and the drugs that she could see. Which leaves us with nothing, except more questions." I hesitated, wondering if I should share the rest of what Celeste had said with him.

"What else?" he asked, sensing my unease.

"She said we're connected, you and me, in a way she can't

untangle." I looked up at Marcus. "She said what you're pursuing is treacherous and that you're dangerous."

"I am dangerous. I suppose it's good to have someone like the Oracle confirm it for me." His voice full of bitterness, he pulled away from me, leaning against the house.

"I don't think she meant it like you're taking it, Marcus," I said, suddenly annoyed at the large chip on his shoulder that seemed to colour our conversations. He was taking a rather vague warning so personally.

"I doubt that."

"Not everyone thinks you're evil incarnate—she was warning me you're mixed up in something dangerous. If you want to take it as a personal affront, that's your own idiocy talking." I was tired and frustrated. This had not gone the way I expected, and now all I wanted to do was go home. I grabbed my bags, slinging them angrily over my shoulder, and headed inside.

Chapter 21

I left Marcus to stew on the bench outside the small cottage. My patience had run out, along with my energy. Everything my mum had said filled my head. I felt like I had more questions now than when this whole thing had started. I headed to the kitchen to find a bottle of water. Taking a long drink, I admired the small space. It had been updated since I had last been there. There was a large open main floor with a small stone fireplace. The bedroom was open to below in a loft above the main space. I put down the bottle and dragged myself up to the loft stairs. Flopping down on the massive four-poster bed, I pulled off my sweater and dirty jeans, leaving them haphazardly on the floor. Marcus could sleep on the damn couch downstairs. This bed was mine now. I curled up under the soft quilt and was asleep in seconds.

Shuffling noises woke me from my exhausted sleep.

"Marcus?" I said, sleepily rubbing my eyes. Moonlight filtered through the open window, casting long shadows on the floor. The earlier clouds had fled, leaving the night clear and calm. I sat up, pulling the quilt around my shoulders. The window was ajar, and the breeze coming through was chilly. Marcus's silhouette appeared in the bathroom door, towelling off his wet hair. The bright light made me squint as I sat up, pulling my knees to my chest. He reached behind him to turn it off. I finally saw him clearly: dressed for bed, shirtless, in nothing more than sleep pants. Despite my earlier annoyance with him, it was hard not to appreciate the view.

"Sorry, I didn't mean to wake you up. I needed to shower off the sticky fingers of the Brownies." he mumbled, walking over to me and sitting on the side of the bed, too close. I could feel the heat of his skin making me shiver.

"You're done sulking?" I said.

"I wasn't sulking."

I raised an eyebrow in disbelief.

"Well, not a lot anyway." He dragged a hand down his tired face. "I hate being reminded of what I am. Even more so coming from someone with as much power to see the truth as your mum."

"I know," I whispered. "But it's not all that you are, Marcus. Stop letting it get to you."

I breathed in the scent of his skin, clean from the shower, with just a hint of the spice I associated with his soulless magic. Unable to resist, my fingers danced across his bare chest. Marcus sucked in a breath at the contact of my icy fingers. He caught my hand in his and looked at me longingly.

"Get some sleep—it's still late," he said.

"No." We had been dancing around each other for days, and I wanted it to end. I wanted this. I wanted him. Even if it was just for a month or a week or just tonight. I sat up, freeing my hand from his grasp and wrapping my arms around his neck.

"Alena," he groaned in warning, his control fraying under my attentions. "You heard what Celeste said. I'm dangerous."

"So am I. You're not that special," I whispered before our lips met.

Marcus held back for a moment before his restraint snapped, and his tongue demanded more from my mouth, exploring. He pulled at the quilt that separated us and slid a warm hand under my shirt. As he slowly rubbed a thumb along the underside of my bra, I arched my back so he had better access.

"Aren't you always the one who's preaching to live in the moment and worry about tomorrow later?" I teased, kissing a trail down his neck, nipping at his ear. He growled at me. It seemed I was getting to him. Interesting. I bit him harder, listening with smug satisfaction to the rumble of approval from deep in his chest.

"Are you sure?" His tone was darkly serious as he pulled back to look at me properly, searching my face to confirm my certainty.

"Gods, yes."

At my words, he set to work on my remaining clothing with unrestrained abandon. I gasped as he made quick work of my bra, palming my small breasts and pinching a hard nipple between rough fingers. With deft skills I didn't know I had, I wiggled out of both bra and shirt without missing a beat, tossing them on the floor. He trailed kisses down my neck as his hand travelled slowly up my inner thighs toward the aching heat, while the other gripped my hip, pulling me toward him.

He slid his thumb and finger under the soft fabric of my panties and plunged the latter into my wet centre while simultaneously rubbing his thumb on my clit. My breath hitched up a notch as I edged closer to orgasm. It had been so long my body needed little encouragement.

I unthreaded a hand from his neck and worked it around to the front of his sleep pants. Gripping his hard, smooth length in my hand, I gently stroked the head with a thumb, evidence of his desire slick on my hands. Stroking him harder, he gasped and growled at me, breaking the kiss.

"Off," I demanded, waving at the offending clothing. He stood, and the pants disappeared. I took a moment to admire him standing there in the moonlight. Eyes ablaze with desire, unashamed of his nudity, he looked every inch a conquering warrior. He grinned at me as I stared. I could see his ego visibly inflating as I drank in the view.

"Like what you see?" he purred.

I rolled my eyes, pulling him close. "It's okay, I suppose," I said, pushing him onto his back. I straddled him, tracing a finger in the divots of his hard muscles.

"Just okay? I'm crushed." His hips moved under me, slowly sliding in the wetness along my swollen opening. I moaned softly as he ground against me, savouring the sensation. He growled as I leaned forward, pushing into him harder. He sat up suddenly, unseating me from his hips, and I lay sprawled out on the bed.

"You're magnificent." He trailed kisses down my chest and lower to the V between my legs. Lowering his head, he lapped at me gently, and I felt the pressure rise in me until it became almost intolerable. The closer I got to release, the slower he went. It was blissful torture. When I thought I couldn't take any more, he rose swiftly above me, a smug look on his face.

I'd had enough of this torture. I pushed him hard with my foot. My surprise attack made him topple ungracefully onto his back again, and I snorted out a laugh at my easy victory. I positioned myself over him and impaled myself onto him with a gasp of pure satisfaction. He bucked under me at the suddenness of it, hissing in a ragged breath. I stilled for a moment, adjusting to the feeling of sensual fullness. His hands gripped my hips hard as I started a slow rhythm between us. His hips rose up to meet me. Flames crept into his eyes as he matched my pace.

"Alena, let go, stop holding back," he said, gripping my hips harder. "Let go."

I hesitated for a heartbeat before relinquishing my control, letting my magic and body be free to just exist without the constant restraint maintained every hour of the day. My magic flared to life at the sudden freedom and burst to the surface. I felt like a dam inside me had burst, power and pleasure intertwined, setting my senses on fire. I embraced it with wild abandon, throwing aside all my doubts and insecurities, lost in a haze of sensation. With a final thrust, my inner muscles clenched around him and I found the edge of the cliff I had been seeking and jumped off it. Seconds later, Marcus roared, and with a final powerful thrust, followed me over the edge.

We collapsed together in a boneless heap of limbs. I watched as our magic mingled with our bodies in tendrils of red, white, gold, and green.

"That's new," Marcus said, watching the magic swirl around us slowly. "Any idea what it means?" he asked, leaving a trail of soft kisses down my neck, making me shiver. He poked at the golden tendrils that whirled along his arms. "This is mine, I suppose, the power of angels, though it's the first time I've seen it like this." He eyed it, fascinated.

"What magic do angels have?" I'd never encountered one. They were rarely seen, keeping to their own realm, similar to the Fae. I vaguely recalled their philosophy of no interference with outsiders.

"I don't really know," he confessed. "I was a terrible student in school. I think it was about healing, matters of truth, that sort of thing." He laughed softly, tracing light circles on my bare stomach. "I should have paid more attention, clearly. It would be helpful now," he said, looking sheepish. "The genuine mystery is the white. That's not something I recognize, do you?"

I did, though I did not know how it had become part of me. "It's the power of seers—people like Mum. Mum's magic looks more like mist, as you saw, but it's similar to this," I said, waving my hand around, watching the white glow follow my movements. "I suppose it belongs to me, though I have no idea how. Perhaps it's because I've been exposed so much to Celeste's magic over the years?"

"I think that's probably impossible." Looking thoughtful, he continued. "Though never say never. With magic, all sorts of strange things seem to happen—more so around you, it would seem. What about your biological parents?"

I had wondered that so many times as I discovered the extent of my magic as an adolescent. I knew so little about my biological parents, and I wished I could have asked questions. I knew it was an impossible dream, but it was lonely as a child not knowing what or how your magic worked.

"My birth mother was human. I never knew my father, so I suppose it's possible. I always thought seer magic was something that only presented in women," I said, frowning at the thoughts of my absent biological parents. I humphed; I wasn't happy about these mysteries. I didn't like not knowing or not understanding something. Even worse, if it seemed to be attached to me.

"Stop it," Marcus said, looking at my frown.

"Stop what?"

"Worrying. It's a mystery, and it bears investigation. Soon, but not tonight." He kissed me softly. "Tonight, is not about worrying about tomorrow," he said, grinning and shuffling closer to me.

I watched our magic swirl and jump, trying not to worry about what it meant in this moment. It was another mystery that would have to wait until tomorrow. Marcus wrapped himself around me, pulling me close under the heavy quilt. We watched silently as our magic danced around playfully. It had a mind of its own, finally delighted to be free. My worries crept back in as we embraced; I couldn't help thinking that this was part of the changes that were barrelling toward me, and I was wildly unprepared.

Chapter 22

I stretched out my happily abused muscles as I lay on the bed in the early morning sun. I had slept soundly for the first time in a long time. Marcus groaned softly beside me, pulling me back under the covers.

"Too early," he said, pulling the quilt over our heads.

"Mmmm, are you sure? There seem to be some parts of you that are up and raring to go," I said, pushing my hips against him, eliciting an entirely different sort of groan.

"No? Still too early?" I said, crawling out from our blanket cave before he could stop me.

He took a half-hearted swipe at me, trying to pull me back to the bed, but I laughed playfully and dodged away.

"Time for a shower then... too bad about you being so tired," I said, turning my back on him and waltzing toward the bathroom door, my bare ass swaggering confidently in the cool morning air.

"Never too early for you," he whispered in my ear, having snuck stealthily out of bed while my back was turned. Damn, that vampire speed was cheating. I shrieked as he tossed me over his shoulder.

"Shower it is, then," he said, landing a playful smack on my ass and carrying me off to the shower. I hoped I might end up actually showered and clean at some point in the morning, though I had my doubts.

We finally made it out of the bathroom after several exciting detours, and I sat at the small kitchen table, looking out over the green fields dotted with sheep and watching the windmills spin lazily in the distance. I dug through my bag, finally checking my phone.

"Shit." I had twelve missed calls from Abby and eighteen texts from Logan. I scrolled through Logan's text messages, getting more excited as I read. Marcus joined me at the table, sliding a coffee over to me.

"What has you so fired up?"

"Logan found a mobile number that our decapitated demon had been calling a few times a day." I slid the phone over to him so he could read the messages, too.

"He's narrowed it down it down to a location, and he's tracking the mobile right now?" Marcus became all business as he finished reading all the texts. "Get Logan on the line. We need to coordinate with Eleonore before we do anything else."

I punched in Logan's mobile number, and he answered almost right away despite the late hour. Marcus pulled up his laptop, getting Eleonore on the video chat to give her the critical information.

"What?" she answered without looking up from whatever she was doing. Eleonore's greetings could use some work, I thought to myself, while Marcus and Logan took turns bringing her up to date on the process we had made.

"Where are they?" Eleonore asked, all pleasantries forgotten, her full attention on us with the news.

"An industrial estate in Cardiff." I could hear the furious tapping of a keyboard as Logan pulled up all the information he had. "It's been there for about three days," he said.

"Shit, that's at least a few hours travel from here," said Marcus.

"You need to come back here to coordinate, and I need this mystery technical person of yours brought in as well to validate this information. I am not going to Wales on a wild goose chase, Marcus." Eleonore's cold barking voice was a bucket of ice water on my earlier good mood.

I shook my head at Marcus. There was no way I was going to drag Logan in front of MCIB. Not all of his methods were considered legal in the strictest form of the word... compounded with Logan being entirely human. MCIB was not known to be the most compassionate with its human counterparts.

Marcus nodded, understanding, though he didn't look happy about it. While he debated plans with Eleonore and Logan, I stepped away from the table to call Abby back. I knew it was the middle of the night there, but several missed calls had me worried.

"Alena? Ugh, what? Do you know what time it is here?" Abby said groggily. Clearly, I had woken her up.

"You called me twelve times. I was worried."

"Oh yeah, that. Two humans were sniffing around the house earlier," she said, waking up properly now. "I scared them off with some flash and bang magic, but I wanted to let you know I'm at Brandon's now." I could hear blankets shuffling in the background as if she was crawling out of bed.

"Brandon's? Really?" I asked, shocked. Those two couldn't get along for more than five minutes in the same room without snipping at each other. Something was very suspect about that statement, but she was safe now, so I would leave off questioning this strange development until I could see her in person.

"Everything okay?" I heard the sleepy voice of Brandon in the background. Yes, this was very interesting indeed.

"Yes, it's just Alena." I heard Abby reply. She started muttering something I couldn't make out to him before returning to the call. "I scared them off with some flashy magic, but I wasn't sure if they'd come back, so I came down to the village just to be safe." She paused. "I think I'll stay here for a few days—keep me posted on what's going on, okay?"

"I will tell you what I can. Go back to sleep—or you know, whatever," I said, not elaborating on what I thought she might be up to. I could almost hear Abby's frown.

"It's not like that, Alena," Abby said in a quick denial.

I grinned, pretty sure it was exactly like that.

"It's not?" came Brandon's unhappy protest in the background.

"Shut up, Brandon. Alena can hear you. I need to go now. Bye."

She hung up on me before I could poke at her further. Unable to help myself, I snickered to myself. I was looking forward to seeing what I had missed at home. Clearly, it was a lot.

Marcus looked up from his call with Eleonore, a question in his eyes. I shook my head, letting him know it was nothing too serious. I could tell him about the snoopers when he was done. I looked around the peaceful cottage, lamenting the likelihood we would be leaving today. I went upstairs to pack and get ready for what promised to be another long day.

After some coordination with Eleonore, we planned to meet her in Cardiff, where the mobile signal Logan was tracking seemed to have stopped moving. We hiked up to the cottage to say goodbye to my family. I was sad to be going, but promised myself I would be back soon.

Marcus walked toward the car with our bags to let me say my farewells without an audience.

I hugged Mum goodbye, noting her tired eyes and the weight she had lost that I had somehow overlooked. I had always known the nature of her gift, but now, faced with the reality of her decline, my heart was breaking. I had to go, but I didn't want this to be the last time I saw her.

Will pulled me into a big bear hug. "Come home soon. It helps her," he whispered in my ear. With a big smile, he released me so Mum could be next to wrap me in a tight embrace.

"Stop it," she said firmly. "I have a lot of life to live yet, so stop looking at me like this is goodbye." Her eyes glazed for a moment. "I will see you again soon," she added with a certainty that made me wonder what else she had seen last night.

I smiled sadly. I would not stop worrying just because she said so, but her assurances helped. Kneeling down to Connor, I gave him a long hug while he made disgruntled noises at the show of affection.

"See you real soon, Sissy and Sissy's friend," Molly waved at me enthusiastically. "Oh, and Sissy, when you come back, can you teach me how to use fire magic?"

I looked down at her, confused, and then at Celeste for clarification, but she just shrugged, unconcerned with the strange statement; toddlers never made much sense, magical ones even less so. I kissed her curly mop of hair. "Sure, sweetie, whatever you want," I said.

I took one more look at my family and turned to join Marcus in the car. I waved through the window once more, and we pulled onto the road, heading for the Edinburgh gate as fast as we could.

The drive to Edinburgh was chaotic. I had been on the phone with Logan several times, trying to maintain his anonymity while sharing information with MCIB so they could transfer the tracking to the technical people there. Marcus was driving at the same time as taking several calls from tactical leaders and from Eleonore for coordination and planning. By the time we arrived, I was frazzled and worn out. It wasn't even lunchtime.

We rushed through Edinburgh's gate to arrive in Cardiff by early afternoon. We had bypassed London, which meant we would have to wait for Eleonore and her team to arrive. We stepped out onto the green public lawn of Cardiff Castle. The gate in Wales was one of the oldest in the UK and was housed within the castle walls. I'd never been to Wales before, and I looked around that ancient structure like a curious tourist. Marcus hurried away, unaffected by the history surrounding us, firing off text messages at lightning speeds.

I hurried to catch up with him, awkward with all the extra baggage, as we hurried toward the car park where our new ride was to have been left for us. I had to hand it to Eleonore. She moved fast. Approaching what I was seeing as the standard-issue MCIB vehicle, we loaded up all the bags and took off toward the mobile signal. We had strict instructions to wait for the backup to arrive, but we would monitor the signal from close by. We pulled into a Tesco parking lot to wait for the others to meet us. Marcus fidgeted in his seat uncomfortably, staring out the window and avoiding looking at me.

"What's wrong?" I asked, reasonably sure this wasn't about the impending MCIB operation.

"When things get going, you know it's going to be an

organized hurricane of chaos. I don't want you to think…" he trailed off. "I… umm." He looked embarrassed.

"Marcus, I get it. It's business time now," I said, trying to shut down this conversation. I didn't want to have the "last night was a onetime thing, please don't be weird about it in front of my boss" conversation. I heard him and his live-in-the-moment philosophy. While I agreed with him in principle, I had no regrets about what had happened between us. However, I would be a lie if I said it didn't hurt to be told it had meant nothing. I didn't want or need a refresher speech. I knew what I had gotten myself into.

He shook his head. "No, that's not what I meant to say. Fuck, I suck at this," he said, rubbing his hands over his hair nervously. "It is going to be all business for a bit, but I have no intention of letting you go when this is over." He pulled me close. "Just don't take off after, okay, at least not until we can talk." He kissed my hair softly.

I didn't know how to take that. Marcus never did what I expected him to do. My unfounded hurt bled away, and I pulled away from him as my phone buzzed in my bag. It had been ringing constantly while we had been talking, but I had ignored it. It was Logan. I put him on speaker straight away, worried something had gone wrong.

"They're on the move."

Chapter 23

"What? Shit," Marcus said. He secured the phone in the holder and motioned for me to buckle up.

"The signal is moving quickly," Logan carried on, "so I assume they are in a vehicle."

Marcus started up the car and peeled out of the parking lot in a shower of dust. "Which way?" he demanded, pulling on to the main road leading out of the industrial estate.

"North toward the highway."

"What about Eleonore?" I asked, aware we were charging into a situation with no backup. The two of us were equipped to take on a large group of unknown, potentially armed and dangerous drug dealers or demons.

"We'll follow for now," he said, handing me his phone, never taking his eyes off the road as he weaved in and out of the traffic. "Get Eleonore on the line and update her."

I scrolled through the phone and called Eleonore.

"What?" came her impersonal voice. Seriously, had she never heard of hello? "The phone we're tracking started moving. We're following it now." My statement was met with silence. "Eleonore?"

"Fuck, we're twenty minutes out from your location." She paused; I could hear her barking orders to someone with her in the background. "This is a shitshow. Fucking Marcus, every gods damn time." I wasn't sure if she was talking to me or just venting. "Fine—follow, but don't engage. Leave this phone connected so we can track you."

I put the phone beside mine on the dash so she could hear everything.

"Just turned onto the highway—headed out of town, I think," Logan said from my phone, which was sliding around on the dash. How could this custom MCIB vehicle not have a phone holder?

Marcus pulled an abrupt U-turn and sped through traffic, following along the route Logan was feeding us. I held on silently, watching the other cars speed by.

"Now they're off the highway. Uh, I think they're headed to the airport," said Logan.

"Fuck!" Marcus bashed the wheel with a hand, pulling off the main highway.

"We're on the way—don't let them get to that airport, Marcus," yelled Eleonore over the roar of the engines.

"Why didn't they go to the gate?" I wondered aloud to myself. "They must be humans, then." Non-magical people avoided the gates. They were more apt to make them seriously ill or fail altogether. It was a small comfort thinking we were speeding toward a group of humans than a pack of demons. Small wins, I supposed.

"Looks like they're headed for the private section of the airport," relayed Logan.

"Go!" Eleonore shouted and then disconnected abruptly. I hoped that meant she was close behind us.

"Turn at the next junction. You should be able to get ahead of them," said Logan. We turned back onto the main road at the end of the runway. There was only one small black car on the road ahead of us.

"That must be them," Marcus said, slowing the car down and letting some distance grow between the two vehicles. With a squall of tires, the car in front of us took an abrupt left turn onto a small side road.

"Shit," Marcus cursed as he cranked the wheel, trying to catch them. The SUV groaned in protest, not enjoying the tight turning radius. "In the back, there's a trunk full of weapons. I assume you've got training?" Marcus spared a glance at me and smiled.

I shook my head as I shimmied out of the passenger seat. The bastard had the nerve to look excited. He was enjoying our little car chase. I climbed into the back seat, trying not to fall as we were tossed around the bumpy laneway.

"Can you shoot out the tires?" he shouted over the din of engine and gravel.

Opening the case, which contained a small arsenal of various weapons, I grinned back at him. I was an excellent shot; I had to be. My magic was useless in combat settings, so I had always pushed myself to be the best with firearms. I had hoped I'd left this part of my life behind me, but I had to admit the thrill and course of adrenaline in my veins was something I had missed. I checked my gun, bracing myself against the back of the passenger seat for stability.

"Good, let's have a go."

Marcus sped up, trying to get closer to them as the window lowered. I propped my arms up in the door frame. My hair whipped around my face. I let the world fade away and focused on the target in front of me. I shot once, twice, as the other car swerved dangerously, trying to avoid us. The third shot connected, and the back tire exploded in a shower of rubber and smoke. The driver veered toward the dense trees and veered off to the left, crashing into the dense trees lining the road. Marcus was out of the SUV and speeding toward the wreck before our car had wholly stopped. With his mighty flaming sword drawn, he charged toward our prey before I could get myself righted. I finally managed to fall out the back door ungracefully and, with my weapon drawn, I sprinted to catch up with him.

The driver had leapt from the vehicle and was running for cover among the trees. Another man stood firm beside the wrecked car, holding what looked like a makeshift potato gun. His stance was confident as he launched a small glass sphere toward us. I watched in horror as the small projectile smashed to the ground, leaving the smell of toxic magic and scorched earth. A cloud of silvery dust floated in the air as the remaining grass smouldered.

Memories flooded my senses. Suddenly I was back in the Kuhbonan Mountains, and I let loose an inhuman scream filled with pure terror. I felt my magic rise as I sprinted toward Marcus. The sounds of my distress had caused him to stop running and look back at me. As another sphere sailed toward us, I pushed myself faster, launching myself at Marcus, knocking him over. I scrambled up and dragged us both away toward our abandoned car.

Marcus pushed back at me, trying to disentangle himself from my insane behaviour.

"I've seen it before—run, just run!" I gasped as the sphere crashed a few feet away and the silver dust crept toward us, shimmering with deadly intent.

Marcus looked like he wanted to argue, but the panic and

fear on my face must have changed his mind. We retreated to the SUV and crouched behind the car, catching our breath.

"What the hell?" Marcus turned to me, anger and confusion warring across his features.

"The silver dust—don't get near it! I've seen it before, even you wouldn't survive," I shot back, angry he was second-guessing my judgement.

Marcus looked out toward our assailant. He had stopped lobbing the deadly spells and was now slowly creeping toward us, giving the scorched patches of earth a wide berth. They were still shimmering with silver haze. He put the launcher down and reached for the gun. His face was dirty and full of hatred as he stalked toward us, intent on ending this confrontation.

"Come out, come out, wherever you are, little freaks," the man taunted. "Let's have a little chat."

I looked at Marcus. He nodded in silent agreement, reading my intent.

I stood up slowly, hands raised. I tried to look scared, which, given the situation, wasn't hard to do. Just because I had seen so much combat in the past didn't mean I was unaffected now. Being unafraid when someone was pointing a gun at you was just stupid. I stepped out from the protection of the SUV, where Marcus crouched, still hidden.

"Oh, there you are... aren't you a pretty little thing? Shall we play a game?" he said. I stared at him meekly. "It's called 'where is your big scary friend?' Because if he doesn't show himself right now, I'll--"

Marcus sped up behind him and removed his head from the rest of his body. I cringed as the body fell. The arm had landed in some of the dissipating dust Marcus stared in horror as the silver consumed the flesh and bone like a ravaging beast until nothing remained but a silver outline on the black earth.

"What is this?" he asked.

"I can't talk about it," I said emotionlessly.

"What the hell does that mean?" I just shook my head, saying nothing.

Before he could demand more answers, I couldn't give him, a line of black SUVs identical to ours rumbled up the laneway and came to a halt. Several armed agents poured out, brandishing handguns, shouting at us to get on the ground and drop our weapons. Marcus looked at his sword and shrugged at me, dropping it on the grass. Another vehicle pulled up alongside the line, and Eleonore emerged, yelling for everyone to stand down.

"Shit—on second thoughts, she looks mad," he said, picking his sword back up and casually throwing it over his shoulder. "Might need this. Come on, let's go meet the cavalry."

I shook my head at his back. He had just killed a man, watched his arm get consumed by magic dust, and was making jokes already. Who the hell had I gotten mixed up with?

Chapter 24

Eleonore surveyed the scene of carnage in front of her with an appraising glare, while Marcus and I stood by our SUV waiting for judgement. She did not look impressed with what she saw. Her phone let go a shrill ring; as she answered it, a maniacal grin spread across her face. It was possible she looked more terrifying when she smiled.

"Good, then this isn't a total loss," she said, shoving her phone back in her jacket pocket and walking past us back to her car. After a few barked orders, the rest of the team withdrew and headed back up the road.

"Come, my little delinquents, time to go home," she said over her shoulder, getting in the car and speeding away down the road. A bemused Marcus stood beside me, watching her SUV disappear around the bend.

"Yep, definitely angry," he chucked to himself, stashing our weapons in the back seat.

"What about all this? It's not safe to leave it here."

"I wouldn't worry—the cleanup crew will be here soon." As if on cue, an unmarked white van pulled up and several hazmat suits piled out, walking past us like we weren't even there. Well, that is spooky, I thought.

The drive back to London was uneventful. I tried to stay

awake, but the lack of adrenaline made me sleepy, and I ended up dozing on and off. Marcus pulled into the car park and stretched.

"What?" he asked when he caught me eyeing him.

"Nothing," I said casually, walking toward the exit.

His arms circled me from behind. "Are you sure?" he whispered seductively.

I laughed. That man was ridiculous. He spun me around, dropping a hungry kiss on my lips that left me breathless. I schooled my face into a mask of impassivity.

"Yep, definitely nothing," I said as I carried on walking.

Marcus laughed. "Tiresome woman! We shall see if we can't change your mind later, then?"

"Perhaps," I said coyly, batting my eyelashes at him. As we approached the elevators for the building, we both resumed our business focus and headed up to the conference room. We had been commanded to attend a debrief to discuss what Eleonore had described as "our various failings." It felt like marching toward the principal's office after skipping class.

When we walked in, I was overjoyed that someone had thought to feed us: along one wall were platters of sandwiches and drinks. I beelined for the table and started loading up a plate. So far, we were the only ones here. As I ate, I watched other agents filter in and take their seats.

Eleonore walked into the room, looking everyone over before taking her place at the front of the room. I zoned out as she went over the procedural elements of the operation and rehashed details I already knew.

"We have one of the human suspects in custody—thankfully Marcus didn't lop his head off as well," she said, sending an annoyed glare in his direction.

They had caught the other person in the car? That got my attention. I sat up in my chair, interested to hear what they had learned. I felt a little thrill of vindication, having already figured out they were most likely human.

"A mage is with him now, trying to extract information from him," Eleonore trailed off for a moment the room was silent. "Conventional methods were not helpful. He seems to have been chanting anti-magic propaganda since arriving here. I think it's safe to say we are dealing with a group of extremists, though the extent of the organization remains elusive. It's a boon to us to finally have someone in custody." Before she could go on, the door opened, and a tired and frustrated-looking mage entered.

"He's dead," he said, slumping into a chair, reaching for a bottle of water, and drinking the whole thing at once.

"What?" Eleonore's rage was palpable. Some of the other agents inched away from the angry vampire.

"I mean, I left for a second to ask the guard for some help and when we returned, he was slumped over, dead. I suspect it was a curse of some kind designed to kill him when activated."

"He killed himself?"

"It would appear so."

"Did you get any more information from him?"

"Unfortunately, no—nothing about who is behind this organization or how large it is… basically, we have nothing."

"Fuck!" She slammed her hands down on the table. "Okay, well, we aren't entirely empty- handed. We need an ID on both of the people who were in that car, and a full analysis of the compounds we found at the scene."

"Alena!" she said, nearly shouting my name.

It would seem I had been lost in my own thoughts for a

second, wondering how this all tied back to the bodies on the lawn and what Mum had said. My attention snapped back to Eleonore.

"Speak. You've seen this silver dust before, correct?" she demanded.

"I have."

"You'll need to elaborate a bit more than that."

"I can't," I said, regret lacing my voice. I really had been serious when I told Marcus I couldn't talk about it. I literally could not. I had been subjected to a spell that bound the information: any attempt to talk about the weapon would cause me to spewing nonsense.

"Try." She looked annoyed.

So, to prove the point, I opened my mouth to tell her in great detail about the horrors that terrified me in the early hours of the night.

"Purple monkey dishwasher," I said, as pain lashed at my temples. I winced; another delightful side effect of the spell was a painful reminder to shut the hell up.

Understanding dawned on her face. "You've been spelled," she said. I nodded, rubbing my temples.

"Interesting. We'll have to find the information another way." Eleonore started pacing the front of the room. "Ideas!" she yelled, clapping her hands as everyone other than Marcus and I started talking at once.

He leaned over toward me, giving my leg a comforting squeeze.

"You okay?" he whispered.

"I'll be okay," I said, looking for my bag, hoping to find some Paracetamol. I glanced at my phone during my search; Abby was calling.

Picking up, I whispered, "Abby?"

I heard Abby's voice on the line, sounding alarmed. "There's another body here… it's bad," she breathed. Panic rose in me.

"I'll be home soon," I whispered, trying not to draw attention to myself.

"Okay," Abby said and hung up. I should never have left them alone, I thought. Someone was still there lurking, and I was half a world away. I needed to get home. Now.

Setting my phone down on the enormous conference table, I noticed the meeting had gone on without me. I sat there processing the fastest way to get home, fighting down my desire to immediately run from the room. Panic wouldn't be helpful right now, I thought.

Noticing my distracted look, Eleonore paused. "Something you would like to share with the class?" she asked pointedly.

I was so sick of this MCIB meeting. I wasn't designed to wait patiently and do nothing. This was clearly their fight, not mine; my people needed me back home. It was time to go.

"No, ma'am—just wondering where the bathrooms were," I said, trying not to show how angry I was with this process.

Eleonore looked annoyed, squashing some of the other agents' snickers. "Near the elevators," she said, waving her hand as if to say I should get a move on, before going back to running the meeting.

"Alena?" Marcus called after me before I could reach the elevators. He looked unhappy, but determined. He pulled me aside to an empty corridor. "Take my car. Call me when you get home—and be safe," he said, handing me his car keys. His words were like a balm on my raging panic. He knew I was going to take off, and he was supporting me. He smiled at me. "Vampire hearing, remember?" he said, tapping his ears and looking mischievous.

I smiled back. "Thank you," I said, reaching up to kiss him hard, not knowing if or when I would see him again. Someone shuffled past nearby, and we broke away awkwardly. I turned to leave, and he touched my arm softly.

"This isn't goodbye," he said, and he chuckled quietly. "Eleonore is a vampire, too. She also will have heard your call." He gave me a roguish grin. "We are going to be in so much trouble when she finds you gone." He gave me another quick kiss before pushing me toward the elevators. I turned and fled before I lost my nerve. Leaving him behind was harder than I liked to admit.

I arrived back in Toronto later than I expected, at nearly one in the morning. Stepping out of the shelter of Union Station, I was assaulted by the wind and rain. A chill settled in my bones as I dashed toward the alley where Marcus had parked the SUV. Something ahead of me moved in the dark shadows. An unsteady reveller from the nearby row of bars staggered around in front of me. I ducked in an alcove to get a break from the driving rain. I went to dash back into the storm when someone pulled me back into the shadows of the building. My hand came up, covering my mouth and nose. I struggled fiercely, trying to get a breath in and shoving against my assailant when I felt a sharp prick in my neck. Before everything went suddenly dark, my last alarming thought was that I could no longer feel my magic.

Chapter 25

I woke up slowly, head pounding out the rhythm of a thousand hangovers. Looking around made my head spin. Where was I? I was bound hand and foot, leaning against a graffitied stone-block wall that had partially collapsed. The room was brightly lit through a bank of windows set high in a concrete wall. Paint was peeling off the walls, and the floor was a mess of broken tiles and dirt. Judging by the light, it must have been near noon. How long had I been out? My captors were standing around a table, just out of earshot. All younger, looking like they were in their early twenties or late teens, they sat listening raptly to an older, battle-scarred man. One of them finally noticed I had woken up. He sauntered over and kicked me swiftly in the hip. I hissed in pain. The bastard had steel-toe boots on.

"Don't look at me like that, freak!" he said, kicking me again before his friend laughed and called him back to the table. Well, they were just delightful company. Searching the room, I assessed the exits. Seeing nothing that would offer an easy escape, I settled in to wait. I reached for my magic tentatively; an empty space was all that remained. That wasn't good.

The older one, who I had deduced was the leader, strode over to me and hoisted me up roughly. Without a word, he shoved me into a cold metal chair. One of the others secured me to it, so I couldn't move. A laptop I hadn't noticed before shone on the table.

"Ready for your close up?" he sneered, walking toward the table. He fiddled with the computer, and then the image of Marcus and Eleonore filled the screen. They did not betray any emotions, but when Marcus's eyes landed on me, his professional mask slipped for a moment. I saw the vengeful angel in his eyes. Whatever happened to me, I knew with certainty in my soul he would destroy these people. The thought warmed me somewhat, knowing these bastards would suffer.

"Listen to me, you contaminated, repulsive creatures. We have one of yours." He waved a finger in my direction. "I think she's a special one too." He leered at me, drawing back and delivering a massive blow to my head. "Isn't she the one you're fucking, Mr Investigator?" He hit me again, harder this time.

I spat out blood onto the dirt floor and tried to look bored. I wasn't going to give them the satisfaction of a reaction. That's what they wanted. Eleonore said something, but the man interrupted her, yelling, "Don't speak! You don't get to speak, filth!" His spittle sprayed the computer screen.

"We want our compatriot back. You know who I'm talking about –you have him in a cell, rotting away like an animal," he said, stalking angrily toward the screen. "I will send you coordinates for an exchange," he spat. He moved slowly toward me with hate in his eyes. "Don't fuck with us, or your special cunt here will be delivered back to you in pieces."

Eleonore glared at him through the screen. If looks could kill, this man would be dead several times over. Her crisp voice came back, finally delivering a shocking statement. "We do not negotiate with terrorists—no exceptions," she said and abruptly ended the call.

My heart sank at her words, though I had expected them. I would have said the same thing. Besides, his groupie was dead. There was no way to give him back, even if she wanted to. I was on my own now. The leader of this little group roared in rage, turning to me to vent his frustration. He sank a meaty fist into my abdomen, and I grunted despite myself, trying to suck in a breath while he landed another hit in my ribs. He rained down abuse on me before pushing over the chair I was on and stalking toward the table, seemingly done with me.

"Take her to the cell block and leave her there," he sneered. "Maybe when she's gone without food and water for a while, they'll be more interested in negotiating." He kicked me in the ribs once more to emphasize his point. The other two people in the room grabbed my arms, dragging me through the hallway. I tried to keep my swollen eyes open, looking for an exit and trying to identify where on earth I was. The long corridor was dark, with peeling paint on the dingy walls. I saw rows and rows of cells. I was in prison? I was wracking my brain for something that might help me. My arms burned in pain as they chose one about halfway down the hall and tossed me on the floor. I grunted with the impact, trying to rise, trying to rise and face them, but the heavy metal door had clanged shut behind me. I had been unceremoniously dumped into the small freezing cell. Before I could stand up all the way, I lost my battle to stay conscious, falling to the floor in a bloody heap.

I woke in fits and starts before finally opening my eyes completely. Surprisingly, I felt no pain from the injuries that had been inflicted on me. My mind was hazy, but even through the haze, alarm bells rang that something was wrong. I looked around the room, which was shades of grey. Sharp corners had been smoothed with a foggy blur.

"Alena?" a voice called, as if from far away. I looked up at the bars of my cell.

"Marcus?" I rose, walking toward him, still shocked at the lack of pain. My senses told me something was very wrong, but I wasn't able to think clearly. Logic felt slippery, and I couldn't quite grasp it. "Marcus? What's going on? Why are you here?" I said,

"I don't know. I'm sorry, I don't understand either," he said. His voice sounded like it was being shouted down a hallway. He faded, becoming transparent for a moment. "I don't know what this is, but I think it's fading—quickly, tell me what you can about where you are," he said urgently.

The emotion in his voice short-circuited my brain, and the pain in my body rose, announcing the injuries that were still there. The brain fog cleared, but as the pain built, Marcus's form faded more. I groped for details of my captivity, trying to formulate something coherent before I lost the opportunity.

"I'm somewhere cold. It's night here—it looks like an abandoned hospital or prison to me," I shouted as the last of Marcus's shadow faded. I let out a sob of frustration, sinking to the floor and banging my fist on the cold cell bars. I was on my own. No one knew where I was, and no one was coming.

I took a shuddering breath. I could do this. It would take more than a bunch of kidnapping thugs to take me out. I gave myself a mental push, trying to banish the remaining brain fog and fight down the pain. I looked at my hands. I was transparent, too, and fading fast. I could see the floor clearly through my hand now. What the hell was going on? Was I dead? Panic seized me at the thought of being a ghost. Tied to this forever. I watched my hand and then my arm disappear. Before the darkness swallowed me, my last thought was of Kit, hoping she wouldn't hate me for dying and abandoning her.

Chapter 26

Waking up in captivity with a pounding headache was getting old. Mercifully, my hand had been unbound at some point while I was unconscious. The idea of one of them touching me while I was unaware made me want to vomit. I sat up slowly and pushed my back against the wall in my tiny cell. A bright light shone through the narrow window. It was morning. How long had I been there? The days were blurring together.

Well, I was still alive, so that was something—and not a ghost. My dream had felt so real; I tried to recall the details, but they just slipped away. Focusing on the here and now, now, I wiped the blood from my eyes and nose; I did a quick inventory of my injuries. There wasn't much that didn't hurt. Nothing serious from what I could tell, though—maybe a cracked rib or two. My nose might be broken as well. I'd had worse, so while everything hurt, I knew I was still going to function. But I needed to get out of there. The light shining through the narrow window was dim; I must have been unconscious for a while. I reached for my magic again, hoping it would have returned, but there was nothing. I wanted to cry at the loss. Having no magic was like being stripped of my soul. Part of me was just missing.

I snorted. Those idiots there had taken something from me, but what they didn't realize was one of my weaker talents. My military training was going to be much more helpful than growing flowers. Still mourning the loss, I tried to stand and collapsed into a heap. I needed rest. Despite being drugged into sleep, I was still running on fumes. Lack of sleep and food would make me sloppy. I settled back against the wall, my eyes on the cell door. I needed to rest for a few hours—the cover of darkness would aid any escape attempt I could come up with. My eyes drifted closed.

When I woke again, my head throbbed less, and while I ached everywhere, my mind seemed to have recovered from the cocktail of drugs I had been given. I shivered. The temperature had dropped, moonlight filtered through the window announcing the arrival of night. I stood, my legs held, and I moved my body around the small cell, trying to regain some heat and circulation. Gradually, the last grogginess of sleep faded, and I was warmer from all my pacing.

The sound of feet marching down the dank hall jerked me from my meditative pacing. The angry man from earlier and two of his friendly thugs approached my cell. They did not look happy. I stared blankly at them as the silence stretched on. One of the thugs shuffled his feet nervously.

"Nothing to say, freak? We'll let you rot in here, you know?" said the leader. "They aren't coming for you—didn't you hear your boss? You're worth shit to them, even that big guy who is boning you."

I continued to stare. I wasn't going to cower to these morons.

"You couldn't have the decency to die in the wreck—very rude—so now we have to do this another way," he yelled.

These were the assholes who ran us off the road in

Creemore? So they weren't after me. They wanted Marcus. When I didn't react, he kicked the cell door with his foot.

"Tell me what you know, you worthless piece of shit, or I'll come in there and fuck you up some more." The sound of rattling metal echoed down the empty corridor. "Tell us about the investigation."

I said nothing.

"Probably too stupid to talk, right?" he sneered at me, his thugs snickering at his insult.

I rolled my eyes internally and continued to look bored. Saying anything to this angry idiot would just make things worse for me.

"Joke's on you, though, isn't it? You're mortal now, no power at all. Just a freak with no magic," he said.

They had been the ones to strip me of my magic? That was alarming. I waited for him to go on. Despite the dire nature of my situation, I was briefly amused that he was a bad guy monologuing the captive. Didn't he watch movies? You should never monologue.

He moved toward the bars, kicking them again. "Tell us about the investigation!" When I continued to say nothing, he yelled, "We are going to kill every last one of you fuckers! You don't deserve the air you breathe. You've used your power to subjugate humans and treat them like dirt."

He spat at me, missing me by a foot. I stood stone still, saying nothing while he ranted. I was dying to ask questions, to get more information, but I clawed back my curiosity. I wasn't in a position to show him how much I didn't know.

"Ha! Now humans will wipe you all from the earth and take back what's ours. We are the pure ones, uncorrupted by magic!" His speech had turned to fanatical yelling. His thugs caught up in his speech, looked full of rage. Kicking the bars again once more for good measure and turning to his compatriots, he said, "Come on, she's too scared to tell us anything. Fuck this." Spinning on a heel, he marched back down the hallway. I heard the distant boom of a metal door slamming.

Time to get moving before anyone else paid me a visit and wanted to chat some more. Looking around for something to use, all I saw was the skeletal remains of what may have been a bed at one point and a hole where the toilet must have been installed. The cell was barren of anything useful. However, the lock on the door seemed like something I might be able to pick—one of my less savoury skills but nonetheless very useful. Taking a rusty spring from the bed frame, I poked at the lock, trying to get the tumbler to move. I jammed it harder, and the spring clicked and cracked before snapping inside the lock. Fuck. The fear I had been steadily ignoring until now bubbled up, angry at my situation, the lock, everything. I hit the lock with my hand. A small fireball exploded out from my fingers and crashed against the wall on the opposite side of the cell.

Whoa, that was new.

I reached inwardly for my magic. It had returned. I felt it inside me. It had always left me with a flavour of mints when I touched it. My awareness felt something more inside me, something with the spiciness of cinnamon and cloves. I reached for it tentatively. As I pulled more, my arm and then my hand glowed a faint red colour. Red? My magic was green. The only magic that was red was that of the soulless. Had I stolen Marcus's magic somehow? Was that even possible? I let the thread of magic go and sat down. The effort of calling it to the surface had sapped my energy, but I could use this. Soulless magic was much more powerful than that of a witch. I wracked my brain for what I knew of it—fire, heat, strength, speed, healing and hearing. It was apparent to me as I sat on the floor in a sore heap that I hadn't developed the healing abilities. But I had fired, so it was time to test if I had heat.

Gripping the metal bar of the cell near the bottom, I reached for the spicy magic again and thought about feeding the magic into the metal. I watched with glee as the metal turned from dull grey to orange as it heated up. Black spots danced in my vision the harder I pulled on the magic; letting go, my arm dropped like lead to the floor. I panted hard, trying to banish the unconsciousness that tugged at my mind. The magic took a lot out of me when I used it. I was only going to get one shot at this. What was the saying, I thought, as I stood up, bracing myself against the far wall—go big or go home? Sure, that sounded right. Time to go home.

Chapter 27

I spooled my magic again, feeling the energy collect in my palm, letting it build. I focused on the thread of power, pulling harder than I had before. When I saw black creep in the side of my vision, I let it go with as much force as I could muster at the door lock, watching as the heat made the metal glow with magic. With a loud clunk, the metal released, and the door swung open a crack. I fell to my knees, sucking in deep gulps of air, trying to banish the dizziness. This would be a very inconvenient time to pass out. Standing, I held the wall unsteadily before taking another breath, pushing off, and propelling myself toward the cell door. I felt a little more stable with every step, and I jogged as quietly as I could down the dark hall. I paused at the corner, making sure it was clear of my kidnappers. Seeing a dim light, I followed it to find a dirty window mercifully open in one of the cells. This one was large enough for me to squeeze out.

I dropped over the other side of the fence, landing awkwardly on the frozen ground. I heard my ankle snap, and I stifled a scream as I sank to the ground. Fuck. The shouting coming from the compound was growing louder and heading this way. I struggled to stand, leaning heavily on the wire fence. Sucking in a breath as I put weight on the ankle, I pushed the pain away and hobbled across the grass toward the line of trees I could make out in the fog. Each step felt like walking on shards of broken glass. Reaching the trees, I heard them shouting behind me and, shoving the pain and panic aside, I looked around. There was no way I could outrun them like this—I needed to hide. I staggered further into the tree cover. The birch trees were thick and slowed me down. I leaned on a tree, catching my breath.

Going forward wasn't working—time to go up. Catching sight of a low branch of a pine tree, I heaved myself up, grateful I had maintained my army-acquired strength. I climbed a few more meters up the tree, wedging myself into the crook of two branches in case I lost consciousness. I did not want to add falling out of a tree to my already long list of injuries. Pulling my inadequate jacket around my shoulders, I shivered and settled in to wait. I could hear my captors yelling, searching the woods for me. I just hoped none of them had the sense to look up.

Hours that felt like a lifetime passed. I had stopped shivering some time ago, and all that existed was the throbbing of my ankle. There had been some close calls in the night, but it seemed they had given up the search. I knew I needed to move soon or face dying there in the tree from hypothermia, and with the first signs of dawn, the temperature had dropped again. I edged my way out of my nook in the tree, contemplating how to get down without inflicting more damage to my throbbing ankle.

I tensed, ready to crawl back to my hiding spot, as I heard someone crashing through the bush. Watching for where the sound was coming from, I spotted a tall, dark figure I would have recognized anywhere.

"Marcus!" I tried to yell, but it came out more like a croak.

"Alena! Thank fuck," he said, finally looking up and seeing me in the tree.

"What are you doing here?" I asked, remembering Eleonore's harsh words from earlier.

"I'm here to rescue you. Obviously, the calvary is about ten minutes behind me." He paused. "I could feel you close by." He looked as confused as I felt by that statement.

"I'm a self-rescuing princess," I shot back.

"You're a hypothermic, injured princess stuck in a tree," he said, pulling himself up beside me and wrapping me in his coat.

I put my arms around him, soaking up the warmth of his body. I shivered violently as he picked his way down the tree, careful of my various injuries. Once he was on the ground, Marcus pulled a radio out of a pocket.

"I've got her." He said in to the staticky radio.

"Acknowledged," came the crackly reply.

We sat on the ground, locked together, as I continued to shiver in the low light of dawn. Before the sun had cleared the horizon, a group of fatigue-clad agents appeared through the bushes. Eleonore was at the head of the group. She looked relieved to find us in one piece. The rest of the small group fanned out around us, waiting.

"I hope you've learned something from this little adventure, Miss MacKenzie. I think the moral of the story here is don't run the fuck away and act the vigilante like a moron," she said, hands on her hips and eyes full of righteous anger.

"Told you she would be pissed," Marcus whispered in my ear.

"Shut up, Marcus," she chastised him, though the words

didn't sound angry anymore. "Let us get Alena back to the road. We have paramedics on standby," she said, more to the group than to us. As one, they moved toward the way they had come from. Marcus heaved me up, following them. Eleonore fell into step beside us.

"What about the kidnappers?" I asked.

"We sent a strike team ahead to apprehend them. The description Marcus provided of your location proved to be more helpful than we thought." She narrowed her eyes at me. "However, how the two of you were able to communicate will require some explanation. Marcus was light on the details," she said, shooting Marcus an annoyed glance.

As her words sunk in, my head was spinning. That hadn't been a dream? How the hell had it even happened? I had heard of people communicating in dreams, but it was rare and not an ability I had. I looked up at Marcus for an explanation. He shook his head subtly, as if to say this wasn't the time. He was right. We needed to talk about how I had stolen his magic—and how we had managed to speak through dreams—but I wasn't in great shape to sort through all the strange things that were happening.

A thought hit me. "They have the drugs to make magic neutral," I said in a panic. They could neutralize the strike team with it—they were in more danger than they knew. I wiggled in Marcus's arms, trying to stand up. "They took my magic," I said.

Eleonore shared a look with Marcus. She swore quietly before grabbing her radio and barking commands at various people. "Take her to the paramedics," she ordered, waving her hands at the other agents, who all took off in the direction of the compound I had escaped from.

Marcus picked up the pace, and we arrived at a makeshift camp at the side of the road. He loaded me up in the ambulance, and the paramedics went to work on my various injuries while he stood guard close by. I leaned back on the stretcher, fighting to stay awake. With the immediate danger past, the adrenaline had bled out of my system, and exhaustion was catching up with me. I stared up at the bright light on the ceiling of the ambulance. Before long, my eyes drifted closed, and I slept.

Chapter 28

I opened my eyes reluctantly, not wanting to leave the sweet comfort of sleep, and found I was alone in a hospital room. It was sad and bare of any furniture, the only light coming from the small window set high in the wall. The walls were beige, as was everything else in the room. I sat up, wondering where I was. The act of sitting up made my head spin, so I lay back down. Before I could get up the courage to pull the drip from my arm, a nurse walked in. She looked unimpressed to find me fiddling with the IV line.

"That's full of pain medication and fluids," she said sternly. "I'll take it out if you want, but you'll be in for a world of hurt when the medication wears off."

I considered my options. I decided I would rather be hurting than trapped in a hospital bed, tied to a set of tubes.

"Take it out," I demanded, holding up my arm. With a huff, she complied, pulling everything off and removing the various bandages. With that done, I looked around for my clothing, plotting my escape. My head was starting to be less fuzzy.

"Where's my stuff?" I asked.

She shrugged and left the room abruptly, clearly not going to aid me anymore. Before I could get any further, Marcus strode into the tiny room, making me feel even more claustrophobic.

"You're awake," he said.

Marcus's concern washed over me in a wave. It was almost as if I could feel it within me. I shook off the feeling, and it faded. The drugs I was on were clearly making me loopy.

"Obviously. Where are my clothes?" I wasn't in the mood to be nice. Hospitals were places people died; I was not dying, so I needed to get out of there before I started to panic. I could already feel my anxiety rising, squeezing my chest and making my breaths come in hurried gasps.

"Alena, calm down. I'll get you out of here as soon as I can, but until then, can you talk to me about what happened?" he said calmly.

His voice was making me angry. I didn't want to be soothed. I didn't want to calm down. I wanted to leave. I struggled to get up, leveraging my damaged arms to sit up. I'd walk out of there naked if I had to, but I was leaving. I managed to get the blankets off me and my feet off the bed. I stood cautiously. My legs held for a moment before giving way under me. Fuck.

Marcus caught me before I could hit the ground. He lifted me up and placed me back on the bed. I struggled out of his grasp and shoved him away.

"Marcus, no talking. Get me the fuck out of here. Now," I cried, nearly in tears. I would not cry in front of him, and I would not stay here. I went to try and get up again.

Marcus put a hand on my chest. "I'll get a wheelchair and some scrubs from the nurses," he said softly. "Can you hold off on trying to escape again until I come back?"

I nodded dolefully, still fighting back the tears, my panic raging unchecked through my body. I watched him go and tried to focus on my breathing. I closed my eyes and counted my breaths as they came. Slowly, the panic receded—not gone, but tamed from the earlier tempest. By the time Marcus reappeared with a bundle of clothing, I had regained enough composure that I was getting curious about what I had missed since passing out in the ambulance. I didn't even know what day it was. Did Abby and Kit realize I was okay?

Marcus watched silently as I struggled into the scrubs, wincing at each movement, but wise enough to let me get on with it without offering help. As I struggled with the clothing, I barked out questions at him.

"Kit? Abby? Okay?" I asked breathlessly, finally getting the pants on.

"Everyone is safe at Logan's. I spoke with him about an hour ago."

"How long was I out?"

"Half a day."

Half a day? Shit. I guessed it could have been worse.

"Bad guys?" I asked, grunting with the effort of getting the shirt over my head.

"Got away. They knew we were coming," he said, helping me put my arms through the sleeves. I decided in gracious mercy not to yell at him for helping me. I wasn't sure I would have managed alone.

"Fuck," I hissed, almost out of energy. Clothing was hard.

"Agreed," he replied. He pulled me to him in a soft embrace, careful not to disturb the bandages.

"You scared the shit out of me," he whispered.

"Sorry," I murmured, swaying a bit on my feet.

Now that I was finally covered, he navigated me to a wheelchair that had materialized nearby. I sat there waiting patiently as he tossed a blanket over my lap. As we headed out the door, a doctor stepped in, blocking my escape.

He held up his hands in defence at my murderous look.

"I'm not here to stop you, though I don't recommend leaving," he said. "I just brought an AMA form for you to sign and some records of your injuries in case you seek medical help elsewhere. That's it." He placed the paperwork on the bed and waited for me to scribble my name on the forms. Backing away from me like I might bite, he walked swiftly down the hallway, out of sight.

"You're scaring the staff," Marcus whispered in my ear as he wheeled me toward the elevators. "Maybe don't do that? They did help you after all."

I tried to school my face into something that wasn't an angry scowl. I was breathing easier as we navigated through the sliding doors stood under the overhang. The building's green and chrome walls reflecting the bright light us as Marcus pushed me to a nearby bench. The sun's warmth shone in my face, a welcome addition to my freedom.

"Better?" he asked, watching me.

I nodded. I didn't want to talk about my almost panic attack or my fear of hospitals. "Where are we?" I asked, changing the subject to something not about me.

"Sudbury," he answered, though he looked like he wasn't quite ready to let the topic of my health status go just yet. "You sure you're okay to leave?" he asked tentatively.

There it was again, the press of worry that wasn't mine. I looked at him to see if he was doing something strange to make me feel this way, but he just looked back at me with concerned eyes, waiting for me to answer. I was questioning if it was the drugs or something else. I needed to get away from this place. It was clearly doing a number on my head—I couldn't think straight.

"Yes," I replied, giving a look that dared him to argue with me. I was not going back in there.

Marcus nodded, though he didn't look happy about it. He pulled out his phone and fired off a few texts while I looked around. The day was sunny and bright, a stark contrast to the situation I had just endured and my dark mood. Pain and exhaustion snaked their way through my body, too persistent to be ignored much longer.

"So, what now?" I asked, hoping he had a plan.

"Now we meet up with the others. They're camped out at a nearby hotel," he replied, not looking up from his phone. "Eleonore wants to do a debrief later today. You'll need to be there as well."

I nodded, getting the sense he wasn't happy about a lot of what was happening today. Marcus rubbed his face tiredly and put the phone down, looking over at me. I wondered when was the last time he slept. It looked to me like he was in the same clothes as when he had found me.

"When this is over, we need to talk," he said. Marcus looked like he was slowly being crushed under the weight of the world. Now that I was no longer feeling helpless in a hospital bed, I went through everything that had happened. New powers that I may have stolen from him, sharing dreams, weird feelings that were definitely not mine—where had all this come from? I had a million questions and no idea where to start looking for answers.

"Yeah, we do. Things got weird, fast," I said, looking at my feet.

He huffed humourlessly, "That's one way to put it."

A black car with tinted windows pulled up in front of us. "This is us," said Marcus, helping me out of the wheelchair. I limped toward the car, trying to maintain as much dignity as I could while still leaning on Marcus. Once inside, I let out a breath, glad I had made it but not looking forward to getting out again. The drive was short and eerily quiet. Our driver did not introduce himself nor say anything, so I sat watching the scenery go by. There wasn't much to see.

The trip from the car to the small hotel conference room was about as much fun as getting in the car. At some point, I would have to get some crutches or a quality healing potion if I wanted to stay mobile. We arrived as the briefing seemed to be wrapping up. Eleonore stood at the front of the room, ignoring us while we slipped in. I hugged the wall for support while everyone else was dismissed and filed out of the room.

Eleonore waved us up to the front as the last person left.

"You shouldn't be up and moving around," she said to me without preamble.

"I'm fine," I said.

She looked at Marcus for confirmation.

"She's fine."

"You're being stupid, and you're helping her be stupid."

Marcus shrugged, unconcerned with her comment. "You try to tell her what to do. It's like talking to a brick." I was grateful he didn't mention my earlier meltdown.

"Fine, well, you're here now—might as well get started. You—the incredibly foolish one—start at the beginning, and don'' leave anything out." She pointed at me with a perfectly manicured nail.

I launched into my version of events as she paced the room, making me dizzy. Looking down at my hands to stop the room from spinning, I skipped over my newfound abilities, unsure of what the implications would be for me, and likewise glazed over the dream-sharing between Marcus and me.

"No. Stop. Look, I'm not blind," said Eleonore. "I can see something is going on with you two, and frankly, I don't care." She paused in her pacing to look directly at us both.

Marcus had been uncharacteristically quiet through my retelling, but he was paying rapt attention now, waiting, it seemed, for the other shoe to drop.

"However, if it is of strategic value or can aid me in any way, I want to know about it. How are you two communicating like this? Don't try to gloss over it this time." Eleonore looked pointedly at me.

"I don't know," I said.

"And you? Thoughts?" She pinned Marcus under her gaze, waiting for an answer.

"I don't really know, but I have a few ideas." He looked over at me as if weighing his words. "Dream walking is an ability that's not unknown to the soulless. However, it rarely appears until after one has met a suitable mate. Why it's surfaced now, I do not know—Alena is a witch, and I have no mate," he said slowly, as if sharing this information was not something he was wholly comfortable with.

"Interesting," Eleonore said, before starting up her pacing again. "Carry on." She waved her hand at me.

I finished my story at the point when Marcus had found me in the tree. Eleonore stopped and sat in front of us.

"I have some questions," she said.

It seemed we had moved to the interrogation portion of this meeting. I braced myself.

"Is your magic gone still, or is it returning?" she asked.

The question surprised me. I hadn't even thought of my magic since I had woken up. I closed my eyes and concentrated on the pool I envisioned when I felt for my magic. I was shocked to find a raging torrent of power flowing inside me where once there had been a calm pool. I felt it bubble excitedly as I touched it with my mind, and it leapt up, responding to the slightest tug. No longer just the cool mint, but the warm spice as well—that was going to need some explanation. Had I stolen it from Marcus somehow, or was it an aftereffect of the drugs?

"It's back," I answered, not wanting to elaborate on the increase of power or the new abilities I seemed to have.

"Good. We had a hunch that it might only be a temporary effect, but you were the first to be dosed and survive, so now we know for sure." She got back up and resumed pacing. How did she have so much energy?

"Any idea why they've been targeting you with these bodies?" she fired at me.

"No idea", I replied. I still didn't have the faintest notion of how this was connected to me.

"I don't like that this is escalating," said Eleonore. She got up and started pacing again. "I don't like that it's grown beyond what we knew about in London and beyond our control." She stopped wearing a path in the carpet long enough to look at me. "I don't like that you are hiding the identity of your rather talented hacker friend from me," she said, glaring at me coldly. Her anger washed over me. I would not give Logan up just because she was staring daggers at me.

Eleonore came back to the table and sat. She leaned back, finally looking tired. For the first time, the mask of professionalism slipped from her face.

"Marcus, you will go back to wherever Alena came from to make sure that nothing was missed. I don't like that someone was still sniffing around while she wasn't there."

Relief at her words flooded me, and this time I wasn't sure if it was just mine or Marcus's I was feeling as well. We needed to sort this out soon. It was freaking me out.

Marcus nodded without comment, his expression unchanged. I wondered briefly if it was just me who was struggling with the strange emotions. Regardless, I was glad to know I was headed home. While I had heard from Marcus that everyone was okay, I wanted to see for myself.

"We will leave for the Toronto gate in an hour," she said as she got up and headed for the door. She paused, sighing dramatically. "Marcus, you need to talk to Emiline about your situation. I'm hardly one to pass judgement, but she's going to find out, eventually. Better it come from you first."

"No," he said with so much finality, I was instantly curious. Who was Emiline that she could bother him so much?

"Suit yourself, dumbass—I'll bring popcorn for when she gets a-hold of you," she said with a laugh before walking out of the room. It didn't sound like something a boss would say to an employee. I wondered what the history of these two was. I looked at Marcus questioningly. He frowned, clearly grumpy at Eleonore's words, and my piqued curiosity.

"This doesn't leave this room—it's not common knowledge, and I'd like to keep it that way," said Marcus.

My eyebrows crept up with curiosity.

"Eleonore is my half-sister, my very annoying, meddling baby sister," he huffed. "She takes great delight in telling me what to do, too." He stood, pulling me to my feet beside him. "Come on, let's get you to one of the cars. It's going to be a long drive back to Toronto."

I still wanted to know who Emiline was, but apparently,

sharing time was over. I saved my plethora of questions for later and hobbled beside Marcus, glad to be finally going home.

Chapter 29

The drive back to Toronto was a long one, but five hours later, I was standing in front of a tall glass condo building. I clutched my bag that luckily had been retrieved from the kidnappers' camp and returned to me. The building, with its modern features, was a stark contrast to the squat stone building of Gooderham & Wort's Distillery beside it. As Marcus spoke to the driver and unloaded the bags, I looked around. It was early evening, and the dinner crowd was turning into the drinking crowd along the central part of the district. After everything I had just been through, it seemed surreal to me that I could stand on the street and watch all the normalness surround me, somehow unchanged.

I had snacked and dozed on the way there, but I was still barely upright. During the drive, I had also reviewed the papers the doctor had given me, glad to see my injuries were confined to bruises and scrapes. The exception was my ankle, which was badly sprained. The swelling had overcome my shoe a few hours ago, and I stood awkwardly on one foot on the sidewalk, vowing to keep healing potions in my bag from now on.

Marcus waved off the car and helped me waddle myself inside and into the elevator. He looked me over. It couldn't have been a pleasant sight. Still in scrubs, I was dirty and matted, having had no time to find proper clothes or a shower. We had spoken little on the drive here; he had been on his laptop most of the time, and I was content to stare blankly out the window and mull over my recent life choices as my ankle throbbed painfully.

"I can feel your pain, you know," Marcus said tentatively. "It's bizarre. Also, next time I ask if you're okay, remember—I'll know if you aren't." I looked up at him, shocked. How was that even possible?

"How?"

"I don't know."

"I can feel you too." I whispered.

"What?" he looked at me, shocked.

The elevator dinged, and we just stood there. As the doors closed, Marcus jumped into action, helping me hobble out the doors and down the hall. We reached the condo, bumbling through the door awkwardly. Marcus helped me to the ultra-modern sofa in the middle of the room. I ran my hands over the smooth, dark leather, admiring my surroundings. From the thirtieth floor, we had a spectacular view of the lake and the twinkling city lights below. While Marcus procured us some food, I watched a plane land on the nearby island airport. It was spectacular.

"Eleonore is sending over some healing potions, clothes and other necessities," he said, as if reading my mind. Maybe he even was; the thought alarmed me. I wondered how far this bond between us went. I focused inwardly, trying to feel for Marcus and failing. Maybe I was too tired?

"As soon as we get you settled, I'll get us some food, too. I know you're in a hurry to get back, but I think we should rest and get you sorted out before heading the rest of the way."

If he expected an argument from me, he was going to be disappointed. I was on board with that plan. I'd had time on the drive to speak with Abby and Logan, so I felt okay about a stopover tonight. I was dead on my feet and excited to get horizontal somewhere that wasn't a cell, car, or tree.

"Is this another one of the vampire holds?" I asked when Marcus got off the phone.

"It is. Do you like it?"

"To visit, sure, but not to live." I looked around. "There aren't nearly enough leaky pipes or broken floorboards for me to feel at home."

I was adjusting myself on the sofa, groaning as I tried to get comfortable, when the doorbell chimed. Marcus went to collect the packages from the courier; I was really hoping they contained new clothes. Marcus picked through everything, locating the all-important healing potion before setting it on the floor.

"Shower?"

"Gods, yes," I replied, trying and failing to get up off the sofa. Marcus hauled me to my feet and then scooped me up, carrying me to the bathroom. This was considerably less fun than the last time he had done this, I mused. He placed me on the counter, handing me the potion to drink. I knocked it back, glad it tasted much better than my cheaper versions. I felt the effects almost instantly and watched, fascinated, as the swelling of my ankle faded. Eleonore had sent the good stuff; I made a note to thank her for it the next time we spoke. That level of healing was hard to come by.

"Better?"

"Much," I said, hopping down and testing it out. It was still sore but useable. I would still have to take it easy for a few days before it healed completely.

"You need help with the shower?" he asked, his expression concerned.

"Well… I just have been kidnapped and beaten, but I suppose I could muster some energy for you," I said, finally feeling well enough to be cheeky.

I felt a fluttering of exasperation followed by a more minor wave of desire—definitely weird, but not altogether unpleasant, this sharing we were doing.

"Not what I meant, but I'm glad you're feeling better." He dropped a quick kiss on my lips and left me to it.

The shower was the most glorious one I had ever had. The dirt, blood and grime oozed down the drain, leaving me feeling clean and renewed. As I was towelling off, the smells of food wafted in. I tore through the bag, hunting for something to wear, finding underthings, jeans and a T-shirt. I smirked at the cartoon dinosaur in a rowboat on the shirt, the caption reading "I make bad life choices." I couldn't help but wonder if there was some not-so-subtle subtext here. Taking off from London like I had probably counted as a bad life choice. Pulling it over my head, I headed back into the main living space, following my nose to the Mexican takeout laid out on the kitchen counter.

"So, want to talk about what happened? The things we didn't tell Eleonore?" he asked casually, as if that wasn't a big question.

"I think I have stolen some of your powers," I blurted out, not sure how to ease into that revelation.

"What? That's impossible!"

"So is all this," I said, cradling a small flame in my palm.

"That's pretty impossible, too," he agreed, watching the flame dance in my palm. He matched my flame without effort. "I don't feel a lack of power. If anything, it's stronger than before. I don't think you stole anything from me."

He extinguished the flame, and I did the same. We sat there for a little while, just eating, both of us unsure of what to say next. I felt better having showered and having healed the worst of my injuries, but I was still exhausted. New powers, new relationship, additional problems –it was just too much newness for someone who had spent the last years avoiding any sort of change.

I yawned without thinking, and the room swam a little. Marcus stood and picked me up suddenly.

"Hey! My feet work fine!" I protested.

"I know."

"So put me down, you oafish cave dweller," I grumbled, not really that upset with being carted off to the bedroom.

Marcus chuffed out a laugh. "Cave dweller? I'd let you walk if I thought for a second, you'd actually go to bed and sleep without protest. Carrying you is easier than arguing with you right now. It's been a long week. We can argue tomorrow."

It was hard to come up with a counter-argument to that. I hadn't planned on sleeping yet. I had too much to go through. I had so many unanswered questions; I wanted to do some research before I finally slept.

Marcus fell on the bed with me still in his arms and effectively pinned me down with his powerful arms. I squirmed, making a half-hearted effort to escape, but his warmth was soothing. I fought to keep my eyes open.

"Quit wiggling, it's annoying," said a sleepy Marcus.

"You're a jerk."

"A tired jerk… go to sleep," he murmured into my hair. I gave up my effort to fight sleep, letting my eyes close as I snuggled closer to Marcus. Tomorrow was soon enough to inspect the tatters of my life and unravel the mysteries I now faced.

Chapter 30

We arrived at the house to a flurry of excited greetings. Logan, Sofie, Brandon and Abby were standing on the front porch while Kit danced happily at their feet. It soothed my heart to see them all there. After many hugs and a few tears, we all settled down to binge on the pancakes and sausages Brandon had brought up from the village for breakfast. I watched my friends and family trade stories of everything we had missed being apart. I also watched Abby and Brandon sneak less than covert glances at one another as we ate. I was extremely interested to hear what had happened with those two, but it could wait until there was less of an audience. Logan and Sofie drifted off home after breakfast had finished, and Brandon left shortly after to open the bar.

We sat around the living room, sprawled out on the sofas. I was stroking a sleepy Kit in my lap, content with an overfilled stomach.

"So new powers, eh?" Abby asked when I had finished the rest of the story I had held back from the others. I wasn't ready to share yet. I didn't want them to worry.

"I've been thinking—what if they aren't new?" Marcus sat up, stretching, before getting up to pace in front of the fireplace.

It was so reminiscent of Eleonore that I was amazed no one had figured out their relationship already. It was so apparent to me now.

"I think I would have noticed being able to throw fire around."

"Not like that. I mean, what if the drugs you got dosed with changed your magic somehow?"

Abby looked thoughtful. "It's possible they changed the nature of your magic or gave it some sort of boost so you can use it differently."

"The implications of a drug that can repress magic for a few days and then bring it back stronger than before is a frightening prospect." I added.

"It wouldn't explain the dream-sharing, though, would it? That's not magic, per se. It's part of a bond between bound mates, isn't it?" Abby looked at Marcus for confirmation.

He shrugged noncommittally. "I don't really know. It's taboo for a soulless to be with anyone other than another soulless," he said, unable to look at me directly. He turned, as if realizing the impact that the words would have. "Not that I care what anyone else thinks," he said, winking at me.

"Ugh, you two are so disgustingly cute!" Abby made dramatic barfing noises.

"I think what I meant was that it would be hard to find answers about relationships outside of our own kind, since it would be something not openly spoken about. I'll ask around discreetly, but I'm not optimistic we'll find any answers."

"So, what's next then, Scooby Crew?"

Marcus rolled his eyes. "I think we need to make another trip to the fae market and ask some more questions. I think we need to track down whoever's been sniffing around the house as well."

Abby snorted. "That's a pretty weak plan, Sherlock."

"I know. I'm open to suggestions." He slumped back down on the sofa.

"I suppose a bad plan is better than no plan." Abby shrugged.

"I hate to add this on top of everything else, but I have no idea how to control this new supercharged power, either. It pains me to say it, but I'll need some help learning control, preferably before I burn the house down," I said.

"Yea, don't burn the house down; that would annoy me greatly," said Abby.

"I would hate to inconvenience you, Your Highness," I retorted.

Abby flinched subtly at the comment before getting up abruptly. "I'm off to work. You kids have fun and try not to set the place on fire or get kidnapped, or anything, okay?"

"I'll do my best."

After Abby left, Marcus wandered off to the kitchen to do some research on his laptop. I dozed on the sofa but after a while I started feeling lazy. So instead, I went and attacked the weeds in the garden with Kit at my side. I was glad to have something to do that didn't have earth-shattering implications. The excursion and the sun wore me out faster than expected, and after a hot shower, I collapsed into bed early. I felt Marcus slide into bed beside me much later in the night. I briefly spared a bewildered thought about how easily he had become part of my life in such a short amount of time. I fell back asleep with a smile on my face. Not all changes were unwelcome.

I woke suddenly, feeling Marcus tense beside me in the bed. Glad I wasn't the only one to be dragged rudely out of sleep.

We lay there, listening for a moment, when the sound that

had roused us both came again. A thudding was coming from the road. Not loud, but steady. Something or someone was out there. Marcus rolled over, pulling on his pants and sliding his sword out from under the bed. I had thought Marcus sleeping with a weapon was a little excessive, though now I was willing to revisit that stance. I followed suit, throwing on sweats and a pullover.

Marcus motioned to me furiously to stay put. I flipped him off and headed for the door. This was my house. I refused to sit here like a cornered mouse waiting to be protected. I could feel Marcus roll his eyes behind me, following me silently down the stairs.

Abby met us on the landing, Kit coiled around her feet. She looked primed for a fight with her double blades drawn. Our little posse headed to the front of the house to peer out the window. Someone was out there stringing up an enormous mass—too large to be a demon. Abby motioned she would go out the back and sneak up from behind our mystery visitor.

Marcus and I nodded, and we slid quietly out the door. I motioned for Kit to stay at the door and wait. She looked annoyed, but obeyed. I gathered my magic to me, hoping I wouldn't blow myself up. I still could not control the new powers well, still in this case, the added firepower was welcome, even if a little unpredictable.

Marcus drew his sword and approached the shadowy figure. "Hey!" he shouted.

The creature turned to face us finally. Seeing Marcus and I armed and glowing with magic, he gave one more shove to the mass he was stringing up and took off around the corner, fleeing quickly. Marcus pursued. I let him go, knowing our guest wouldn't stand a chance pinched between Abby and

Marcus.

The creature that was looming on a pole in front of me. It was massive and furry. There was no moon tonight, so it was hard to make out the details, but it looked like a moose. I let my magic unravel, reaching my hand out to the moose. I pulled the head around to face me. Its glass eyes and very fake fur looked back at me. It was a freaking massive stuffed moose. What the hell? I let it go, and it flopped back down, looking sad and undignified. Before I could process this new piece of weirdness, a boom followed by a wave of wind knocked me on my ass. I felt tiny shards of wood fly by, nicking my skin in several places.

Getting up, I called my magic back and sprinted toward where I thought Abby and Marcus would be. I rounded the corner and came up short. The far corner of the house was missing. I could see the interior of the old dining room and upper floors through the loose wires and pipes leaking water onto the grass. Looking around frantically for Abby and Marcus, I found them alive and whole, crowding around the giant oak tree overlooking the creek that functioned as a property line. Seeing they were okay, I turned back to the ruins of the house, rushing to the front porch hoping Kit had heeded my words and stayed in the front hall—where she would be safe from the blast. Rounding the corner, I saw her small body in the front bay window. My steps slowed. I waved at her to just wait there, content she would be safe for the moment I moved back slowly to the backyard. As I wound my way through debris, my heart broke. I had no way to make that better, the house was destroyed. Taking a shuddering breath, I heard where the others were standing. Approaching, I saw Marcus had tied our new friend to the tree and was interrogating him as Abby looked on passively.

At my approach, he paused his questioning. The creature secured to the tree was a fae, tall and lean. His beautiful face was crowned with long white hair and his bright emerald eyes glared angrily. He sat on the grass, dressed awkwardly in dishevelled human clothing, a few bruises showing on his too perfect face.

"I told you already I don't know what drugs you're talking about," he snarled at Marcus. "I was here for the princess!" he said, looking at Abby. "Your Highness, please forgive me for the intrusion. I was unsure how to proceed in the human realm," he pleaded. "If I have brought offence, please let me prove my worth to you." He was practically begging by now. I looked over at Abby for an answer. She looked ashamed and miserable.

Sadly, she sighed. "Let's go inside and talk. He is no threat to us," she said, motioning to the angry fae at our feet.

"I'll keep an eye on this one. I still have some questions that need answering," Marcus said, leaning on his sword. The fire in his eyes that had yet to fade.

As we approached the ruins of the back of the house, we paused. "This is all my fault," she said, dejected. "I'll make this all better, I promise."

Abby sunk down onto the front porch, looking miserable. She let out a small moan of pain while hanging her head. Kit burst through the door, all fangs and growling, apparently coming to rescue Abby from whatever was making her groan in pain. She vibrated, bouncing around angrily, looking for someone to attack before bursting into a ball of white fire. Abby leapt up, and I rushed forward, panicking at the sight of Kit engulfed in flames.

"Kit!" I screamed as I tore off my sweater and threw it over her to smother the flames.

Kit's pink nose poked out from underneath it, followed by the rest of her tiny head. She looked up at me, apparently confused at my panic and by being smothered by a sweater.

"You were on fucking fire, Kit!" I shouted, still horrified by the sight. She wiggled out of my grasp and sat on her rump. I watched as her little face shone with concentration before flames leapt up to her body once more. She gazed at her tiny paws in wonder before looking up at us, looking very pleased with herself.

"What the hell?" Abby exclaimed.

I stood watching Kit turn the fire on and off. She was delighted at her new toy, and my panic receded when it became apparent she wasn't in any danger. It seemed like I wasn't the only one with new abilities. What the hell was happening to us?

"The house is doomed to burn to the ground with you two walking torches around," Said Abby.

"Says the person who just blew a hole in the side of our home."

"Fair point."

"So... princess?"

Abby sighed. "I am the third daughter of the Queen of Light, so technically a princess—but I'm not really embracing the role right now."

Queen of Light—that was no small thing. I knew little about the hierarchy of the numerous high courts of the Fae, but I knew the Court of Light was up there in both prestige and power.

"Obviously. What does this have to do with our unwelcome

guest?" I asked.

"I came of age recently, which I guess means I'm ripe to marry off to the highest bidder. It's bloody barbaric and backward."

"Happy birthday?"

Abby snorted. "Somehow, this one found out where I was and started the courting process, which entails gifts, proof of strength, that sort of thing. It's ridiculous. But it explains some of the stuff that's been showing up on the lawn."

"You're just telling me now?"

"I thought I was safe here. It didn't really occur to me. I'm sorry."

I pulled her into a hug. "It's okay, we will figure all this out, including whatever *that* is." I sat motioning to Kit, who was happily prancing on the lawn, leaving minor scorch marks in the grass. I was still freaking out about Kit being a furry torch, and Abby was a fae princess. This was turning into a hell of Tuesday night.

Grumpy muttering alerted us to Marcus's approach. Abby looked like she'd had enough for one night. I had never seen my friend look so defeated before. I was worried about what this meant for her. Was she going to come back to her life here again?

"It's fine. I won't say anything to the others unless you want me to. Go, take little Flame with you before she does any more damage to the lawn," I told her.

Abby scooped up a protesting Kit and disappeared into the house as Marcus rounded the corner carrying the fae, whose mood had not improved with being pushed about.

"I'm going to take him back to London," he said, opening the back door of the SUV and shutting the door on the Fae's loud protesting of this plan.

"Tonight?" I asked, unhappy at the thought of Marcus's abrupt departure.

He nodded sadly, pulling me close and kissing me softly. He broke away, walking past me into the house to gather his things. I waited on the porch, mulling over everything that happened. Marcus reappeared, dressed in his all-black uniform and carrying his duffle bag.

He tossed everything in the SUV before turning to me. I walked over to where he was standing. He pulled me hard toward him, leaning down to brush my lips softly with his own. I kissed him back, demanding more than he could give right now, and then broke away, knowing I had to say goodbye before I betrayed how much his leaving was upsetting me. I don't know why I bothered. He could probably feel it. This pesky bond between us made it hard to be stoic.

"I'll call you?" he asked.

"Sure," I agreed softly, wondering what that meant. I really sucked at this.

I felt his reluctance to leave, mirroring my own. You'd think having a front-row seat to Marcus's emotions would make a situation like this more straightforward, but it didn't.

I watched him drive off into the night, staring at the road long after his tail lights had faded before heading into the house to start my day. Sleep was for people who had everything figured out. That wasn't me.

Chapter 31

I took a deep breath. The night air smelled of campfire and pine. Summer had made a surprise appearance tonight, and the warm breeze wrapped around me like a comfortable blanket. Brandon, Logan, Abby, and I sat around the cheery fire chatting after spending the entire day boarding up the house and making it as safe as we could manage.

The contractors would be here in a few days, but I needed to keep the rain and the animals out until then. In books, you read about the epic battles destroying buildings and levelling cities. No one ever mentions the monumental task of cleaning up after such events. Ours could hardly be considered a battle—the house had borne the brunt of the violence, after all—but the cleanup element remained. Marcus had left with Abby's unwanted suitor that night, conveniently missing this exciting task.

"Have you heard from Marcus?" Abby asked, breaking up the quiet group contemplation, complete with therapeutic marshmallows.

"Nope," I said, trying to sound casual about this, like it wasn't eating at my mind that he hadn't contacted me. I knew what we had was brief, but I thought it would at least warrant a text message or something. Three days later, I was wondering if I had misjudged the situation.

"Why not call him? Clearly, you don't want things to end in mutual ghosting," Logan asked.

I had been asking myself that for a while. The bond between us was still there. It was faint, but enough to tell me he was okay. While it was true I didn't want things to end, there was another part of me that felt this was for the best. Our time together had been intense. Just the memories sent a rush of heat through my body and turned my cheeks pink.

"I might, I might not. I don't know," I said, shrugging.

"Truer words were never spoken," Brandon chipped in.

"Okay, be quiet, you! Like you know anything about relationships," said Abby.

"Oh, Abby, I am deeply wounded by your words. I am a love expert."

Abby scoffed.

"Besides, what do you know of love? Your suitors bring you dead body parts," said Brandon.

I sat back in my chair, glad the conversation had steered away from my love life. Abby and Brandon bickered as if it was a sport. I wouldn't have been surprised if they both had a secret scorecard somewhere to keep track of the numerous arguments they had over the years.

They had both been cagey about what had transpired while I was away, and I took the hint. Whatever was between them, I left them to it. Since I had come back, their relationship had carried on much the same as before. The only addition was the covert glances each made when the other wasn't looking. Logan and I pretended not to see. They would tell us when they were ready.

"I don't think either of you is qualified to be giving advice," I said. "Besides, I thought you two had called a truce since Abby spent the night with you." I could not resist poking at them one more time. I was only human.

Logan looked up from his phone. "You two slept together?" he asked, surprised.

I forgot that wasn't common knowledge.

"No!" they said in unison.

"Right, okay," Logan said, not looking convinced and looking at me for clarification. I just shrugged, feeling bad for bringing it up.

"Humans bring dead plants—which take little skill to ac-quire—or worse, pay another to deliver them. How is that any different, or even romantic?" Abby said, huffily changing the subject.

Logan chuckled. "She's got you there," he said, rising. "All right, kids, you behave. I have to go rescue my babysitter and get some sleep." He waved goodbye and faded into the dark night.

Brandon took a long pull of his beer and glared at Abby. She looked back at him smugly. I had a feeling these two would be at it for a while still. As I was listening to my friends bicker about various romantic traditions, I smiled to myself. Life was good like this.

It would have been better with Marcus, but we would always have the fated mate situation hanging over our heads, just waiting to break my heart. Without him here, things were still good. I could make my peace with that. Tonight, though, I was still grumpy at the lack of contact. I focused on the now heated argument between Abby and Brandon. I rose slowly, still sore from my many misadventures and the added labour of boarding the house up that day.

"All right, I'm going to bed. Brandon, you're on the couch tonight." I gave them both a long look. "Behave yourselves," I said before turning toward the house, the sounds of angry murmuring behind me. I shook my head. Those two were ridiculous.

I navigated through the front hall, which was now overflowing with gifts of all types. It seemed the word was out that Abby was here, and her suitors had multiplied overnight. Thankfully, no more bodies had appeared. That was going to be a Future Me problem. I headed to my bed, taking a quick peek in on Kit. She had been doing better since her magic had appeared, but it seemed to make her more tired than usual. I was worried about her, but unsure of what to do. It was another problem that wouldn't be solved tonight.

I sat on my bed and stared at my phone. Logan was right; it was childish of me not to breach the silence. Taking a deep breath, I typed out a quick text—*I miss you, don't be a stranger*—and hit send before I could talk myself out of it. I lay down, contemplating how much had changed in such a short time and how much there was still to figure out. Sleep did not come for quite some time.

Morning found us all quietly drinking coffee on the porch together. We admired the offerings left overnight by Abby's latest suitors. The piles of gifts had filled the dining room and had now spilt over into the hall. Kit sniffed a box before sneezing and backing away from the package.

"A bunch of yarrow leaves?" Brandon observed. "How is that romantic?" he scoffed.

"I need to put a stop to this. It's becoming absurd," said Abby, throwing her hands up in the air. "I need to go back to court and end this ridiculous fiasco," she said softly, looking defeated.

"You're leaving?" Brandon asked. He sounded genuinely upset at the prospect of her going away.

"Are you sure?" I asked.

She sighed, sounding sad. "Yes, time to face the music, as the humans seem to say." She looked over at our collective misery. "Don't worry, I'll be back, eventually. My life is here—I will not give that up without a fight. I suppose I should go pack." She got up from her seat and went inside without another word.

Brandon looked out at the pile of brightly wrapped gifts and strange packages, lost in his own thoughts.

"Want to talk about it?" I asked.

"Nope." He got up, handing me his empty mug. "I'll see you later. The Meet won't open itself," he said, before climbing into his car and driving away. I couldn't help but feel that my friends were all suddenly drifting away, and there was nothing I could do to stop it. I looked out at the road, wondering what the future held. Things were changing fast, and I wasn't sure if I liked where it was headed.

Later that morning, Abby and I said our goodbyes. Not being ones for sentimentality, we were brief with each other, but sad nonetheless. Having given me her assurance she would be back soon, she strode down the road to take on the fae high court. I did not envy them: Abby was on a mission, and I pitied anyone who tried to stop her.

After a morning of calling contractors and being discouraged by the prices quoted to fix the house, I wandered into the kitchen for some comfort cookies. I saw a note and a large envelope on the counter with Abby's scratchy handwriting on it.

Fix the house, it's not fit for a princess—Abby

I laughed; inside the envelope was enough money to repair the damage. Perhaps if I was careful, it would be enough to finish the house completely. This was amazing. Part of me wanted to give it back to Abby because it was too much, but feeling the breeze come through the makeshift boards, I swallowed my pride. Abby had saved Purple Hill, and now it was time to make it fit for a princess.

Chapter 32

Days bled into weeks. Spring had given way to the long, hot days of late summer. I listened to the crickets in the fields chirping, watching the sun sink toward the horizon. Kit was sitting in my lap, peacefully dozing. We were relaxing in the new porch swing that the contractors had installed today. It had been the final touch on the renewed porch. No more loose boards or peeling paint to be seen. The damage from the battle had been fully repaired, so the house was no longer drafty and full of large holes. We still had a long way to go with the renovations, but I was confident now that it would get done before winter set in.

After weeks of not hearing from anyone for days at a time, I went stir-crazy. One morning, full of entirely too much coffee, I had come up with a plan to create an online potion business. I mixed up hundreds of potions in the space of a week in a flurry of inspiration. Everything from sleeping drafts to acne cream now sat neatly organized in the former storeroom on the second floor, which I had converted into a small workroom. I had launched the website for my new business, appropriately named "Stir Crazy," close to a month ago. Word had spread around the surrounding county faster than I had expected.

Business was booming, and I suspected this was partly

because the village Facebook group was finally being helpful for a change. With my new enterprise going well, I found some financial security that had allowed me to stop worrying about losing the house. I would not make millions, but it was enough to cover the bills. The project had also given me something to be excited about for the first time in a long time. I was making long-term plans and goals. It felt good.

I missed Abby fiercely. The house was too quiet without her. She had called a few times to check in but had been cagey about what she was dealing with, always assuring me she was fine and would be back soon. With fall approaching, I was losing hope this would be a quick trip. Since Abby had left, Brandon had grown sullen, and while he put on a mask of cheerfulness, he wasn't fooling anyone.

People were speculating as to what had caused this strange change in everyone's favourite pub owner. I asked him about it a few times, but he brushed me off. Rather than having him push me away further, I just avoided talking about Abby altogether. It worked out well since I was also utterly unwilling to talk about Marcus's lack of communication. Months had come and gone without a word from him. The time and distance had faded the bond to nothing. Sometimes I could feel something, but I had a feeling it was more my imaginative hoping than anything concrete.

Getting up from the swing, I wandered around the back of the house to check on the garden before it got too dark to see. Kit followed behind me, but stopped at the gate. Her magic had grown, but her control was still lacking. She had been banished from the garden after accidentally lighting several expensive plants on fire. The garden had been expanded to accommodate the ingredients necessary for the potions I was now making each week. I was reviewing the work needed when I heard the sounds of a car arriving in the driveway. It must be the courier, I thought. I had a regular pick up now with all the business coming in. I went around the house, stopping short when I saw who was there.

Marcus leaned up against the SUV, looking casual in jeans and a T-shirt. I was mad at him for the radio silence, but it was hard not to appreciate how good he looked standing there in the late afternoon sun. I had always wondered what he would look like in clothing that was any colour other than black.

"I'm sorry," he said before I could say anything.

As far as opening lines went, that was a good one. I felt my anger fade a bit. I was never one to hold a grudge, and if I was honest with myself, I was mostly hurt he had just disappeared on me without a word. I walked toward him and came to lean against the SUV beside him.

"I'm listening," I said. I was, too. I wanted to hear why he hadn't spoken to me for months.

"I am stupid," he said matter-of-factly.

"No argument coming from me on that point," I said, staring at my feet. I wasn't good at this type of thing. I would rather do anything else but talk about feelings. He sighed heavily, turning to face me.

"Look, I like you a lot—which is uncomfortable for me—so when I got back to London, I threw myself into work, thinking it was the best thing for both of us. Time went by, but it didn't fade. I got your message, and I just felt like an ass for not answering and that I was making a mistake, a big one," he said.

"If the shoe fits," I interjected. I kicked the dirt at my feet like a pissy toddler.

"Look, I'm not perfect. It's no excuse. I'm here now, and I

want to give this thing with us a go. I worry about it ending badly because of what I am. Hurting you would kill me, but I would rather have a short, complicated, and messy relationship with you than none at all. I know it's selfish."

I looked up at his face. His eyes looked tired but hopeful. It was easy to overlook that I hadn't made much of an effort to contact him, either. One text message hardly counted as effort. At the end of the day, I had been pretty complacent about the silence. It was hard to stay angry about something I had more or less also done myself.

I was going to give in. Short, messy, and complicated sounded good to me too. I could feel it. I was an idiot putting my heart on the line like this, but it wouldn't stop me. I understood why he felt this way, because I had the same issues. I didn't want to get attached, just to be left when his mate showed up.

I was also sick and tired of only half living. Hiding up here in my old house was not the person I wanted to be. I had to admit the time apart had given me the space to think about what I really wanted. I wanted to take chances sometimes and damn the consequences. It may end in tears eventually, but not today, I thought. Marcus looked down at me, waiting for me to say something. I let him sweat a little longer, pondering what to say next, so I didn't sound like an idiot. Words were not my strong suit, so I just acted. I took a step toward him and smiled. He wrapped his arms around me, letting out a relieved breath. I tilted my head up toward him, meeting his urgent kiss with all the pent-up emotions of the past month.

"That's it?" he asked. "I had come prepared to fight."

"It's okay. The way I see it, you left and now you're back, and you're really sure you want to be here. It's much better than having stayed and second-guessed your choices."

He chuckled, reaching into the car bringing out a large envelope. "Well, I brought you a gift to soften you up, anyway." He handed me the envelope.

I opened it up and peeked inside, pulling out the documents. Looking them over, tears streamed down my face. They were travel documents for Kit—and more than that, there at the bottom where the legal guardian was listed was my name. Kit was officially part of my family. I was going to ugly cry and just didn't care. This was the best gift he could have ever given me.

"How?" I said, wiping tears off my face.

"You don't want to know." He scrunched up his face. "But I now owe a favour to Eleonore."

I laughed through my tears. This was so much more than I could have ever hoped for. I could finally take Kit to Scotland, or wherever we wanted to go. We were free, and no one could break up our little family.

"Thank you," I said, throwing myself at him and gathering him in a hug.

Kit leapt up excitedly, her flames popping up all over her body.

"Oh fuck, Kit, you're on fire," he said, panicking, pulling off his jacket to smother the flames.

"It's fine. Come on, Kit, turn off the flames. You're freaking him out," I laughed.

Kit concentrated, and slowly the flames dimmed. She looked up at us, pleased with her control of the magic.

"Nice work, buddy, you've been practising."

She pranced away to the porch happily. We followed her slowly up the path, Marcus's face still wearing the expression of total wonderment.

"What was that?" he asked.

"Yeah, you may have missed a few things," I replied.

"A few?" he asked, curiosity lighting up his voice where he sensed a new mystery to be solved.

"Turns out Kit's not just a shifter."

"Not a shifter? What is she?"

"No idea," I said, because it was true. I had no idea what Kit was, but that was a problem for another day.

"No idea?"

"Nope." I grinned at him.

Marcus grinned back as I led him by the hand into the house to show him just how much I had missed him.

***

In honour of our new life of living in the moment, on a whim, we had rented a small cabin on the shores of Lake Huron. We hadn't left the cabin much that past week. I grinned at the memories stretching out my legs. I was sore in places I wasn't aware you could be sore.

Sitting on the end of the dock, I felt rather than heard Marcus sit down beside me. Our bond had come alive since he had returned; it was comforting to have it there but also disconcerting to be tied to another person so intimately.

We were still adjusting. Marcus handed me a beer as we looked out at the lake. The calm peace of the evening seeped into my bones. The night sky shone overhead with a riot of stars, and the late summer breeze tugged at my shirt gently. I leaned into Marcus, feeling his now-familiar warmth through my shirt. There was still so much to work out. How would we make the relationship work? He was on a sabbatical now, but for how long? Not forever. He loved his work. The bigger questions were left unanswered, too, like where my new powers had come from and how to use them. I'd been practising but without much progress. Kit's power, too, had only grown. She showed improvements in her control, but what she was and how to help her were still unknown. I knew these mysteries wouldn't be solved today; today I would embrace the moment of peace with open arms.

I turned my gaze up to face Marcus. The serious MCIB man was gone, and in his place, the real Marcus sat beside me, his intense blue eyes looking back at me as a smile tugged at his lips.

"What?" he whispered as he lowered his head to mine, gently brushing my lips with his.

"Hmmm, this is good," I said as I reached for him, deepening the kiss.

"Good? That's all, just good?" He chuckled. "Room for improvement, then," he said, as he picked me up in one swift movement and placed me gently on my feet. He pressed his hard body against mine.

Marcus stiffened suddenly; a shudder passed over him, and he hissed a cry of pain as he grabbed at his wrist. "What the hell?" he cried. Looking down at his arm, we saw one of his bound tattoo rings slowly fade. My alarm rose—that shouldn't be happening. He looked at me, the blue eyes replaced with bottomless black pits, his face blank. He struggled for a moment to regain some of himself briefly. "Run!" he croaked out.

"What? No, what's going on? Tell me!" I demanded. I wasn't just going to run from him. I'd only just found him again. This was insane.

Marcus reached for me, violently shaking me before roaring,

"RUN!" His eyes held the smallest of flames, but it was growing. He vibrated with energy, struggling to maintain his composure. I watched in horror as his face morphed, eyes aflame, fangs descending. He was gone. In his place was a monster.

So I ran.

Candlelighters

A portion of all book sales goes to support Candlelighters in Ottawa, Canada.
Candlelighters is a local, not-for-profit organization that provide programs and services to young cancer patients, and their families, receiving treatment in the National Capital Region.

For more information visit candlelighters.net

About the Author

Ember Russell grew up in rural Ontario, on the shore of Lake Huron, where she spent most of her youth making a concentrated effort to become a pirate. When that fell through, she joined the circus, travelled the world, failed at several careers before settling in Toronto to work as a Person Friday, a title she still doesn't quite understand. She took up writing when she discovered that she had finally reached the bottom of her book pile, figuring writing was just reading in reverse.

Discover more by Ember Russell

Creemore Series
　Soulless – Book One
　Unbound – Book Two (April 12, 2022)

Connect with Me

Twitter @EmberRussell1

Website: www.emberrussell.com

9 781777 767419